AF271148

had a habit of jealously guarding that part of his acquaintance which lay outside the immediate world of ballet—he always had done, right from the very earliest days. It had been the source of some of her most bitter resentment, her most deeply felt hurts. Nicky's friends had never been her friends. Nicky had gone off by himself, done things without her, never thought to take her with him even when he might have guessed that she was eating her childish heart out to go. That was the way he had met Vic: jauntering off one summer holiday on some overland trek in a minibus to the edge of the Sahara desert, leaving Gill to stay behind in Clapham with Nanty and with Alex. She had cried over that. Alex had tried to reason with her, pointing out that it wasn't fair to expect Nicky always to include her in everything that he did, that he must be allowed to have a life of his own, independent of the family. She had known Alex was right, but still she had refused to be comforted. She *could* have gone on the minibus: there were girls as

well as boys. Mixed party, it had said—
she had seen the brochure. Fifteen to
thirty-five. Well, *she* was fifteen. There
wasn't any valid reason why she shouldn't
have gone. It was mean of him not to let
her.

It wasn't mean, of course, she could see
that now; but still some of the hurt
remained. It was unimaginable to her that
she should ever want to do things without
Nicky, that she could ever have a circle
of acquaintance from which he should be
excluded. It had been almost three years
before she had been allowed to see Vic—
and then he hadn't been in the least bit
as she had pictured him. He had been
quite old, for a start—at least thirty if he
was a day—tall and shambling and big-
boned, with a bushy beard and hair the
colour of straw and large, punchy face
like that of an amiable carthorse. She had
liked him at once, and he had seemed to
like her. He had agreed that it was
nonsensical of Nicky not to have intro-
duced them long since.

"But then," he said, "that's Nicky for

MASQUERADE

Alex, Gill, and Nicky, the three brightest talents in the New London Ballet, brought up together as children, were still inseparable friends. When Nicky and Gill won leading roles in a new ballet, Alex realised that Gill was eating her heart out for Nicky, who treated her as a troublesome kid, and made it clear that he already had a secret lover. Gill's dancing suffered. Even reliable Alex, pursued by the sexy French ballerina, Danielle, was no comfort. Gill began to doubt herself as a dancer and a woman, as Nicky's hidden life emerged . . .

Books by Jean Ure
in the Linford Romance Library:

HAD WE BUT WORLD ENOUGH, AND TIME
NO PRECIOUS TIME
MASQUERADE

JEAN URE

MASQUERADE

Complete and Unabridged

LINFORD
Leicester

First Linford Edition
published March 1990

British Library CIP Data

Ure, Jean, *1942*–
Masquerade.—Large print ed.—
Linford romance library
I. Title
823'.914

ISBN 0-7089-6830-9

Published by
F. A. Thorpe (Publishing) Ltd.
Anstey, Leicestershire
Set by Rowland Phototypesetting Ltd.
Bury St. Edmunds, Suffolk
Printed and bound in Great Britain by
T. J. Press (Padstow) Ltd., Padstow, Cornwall

1

FOR three months, the New London Ballet had been on tour: for three months the Theatre-in-the-Strand had echoed to alien sounds. Wagner had displaced Tchaikovsky, moth-eaten mechanical swans been dragged back into storage, rows of delicately fluttering snowflakes given way before the savage onslaught of the Valkyrie hordes. Where scrawny ballet girls in leotards and tights, hair pulled back into virginal buns, had clopped up the stairs in their blocked pointe shoes and sprawled ungainly, gossiping in the dressing rooms, the ample ladies of the opera had sailed stately instead: where young male athletes, with bodies well strung and lean thighs muscled, had sweated and strained and achieved miracles of physical impossibility, big bass baritones had stalked imperious and tenors like pouter pigeons sung the glory of Isolde. Now, very soon, the positions were to be reversed; it would be the turn of the opera to pack up and move on. The rightful inhabitants had already come back—back, at any rate, to London, if not yet actually to the theatre. One half of the Company had arrived yesterday afternoon from Manchester, the other half were arriving this evening from Istanbul. Rehearsals for the new season were scheduled to start first thing the following Monday. It gave but a five-day break for aching limbs and protesting sinews, but as the more philosophically minded pointed out, five days was five days. It was better than a poke in the eye with a burnt stick. The less philosophically minded were more inclined to agree with Nicky and his heavily sarcastic: "Five days! Big deal!"

They were in the airport lounge at Istanbul awaiting the flight announcement at the time that he said it. They had been in the airport lounge awaiting the flight announcement for what seemed eternity. Nicky, who wasn't very good at waiting at the best of times, and least of all after a strenuous three-month tour over half the Middle East, had already paced twice round the perimeter, read out loud the contents of every newspaper and magazine he could lay hands on, drunk innumerable cups of airport coffee and talked everybody into a near coma. Now he threw himself moodily on to the bench next to Gill, hands in pockets, chin sunk in sweater, legs flung out before him. For a few blissful seconds there was silence, then: "At this rate it's going to *take* us five days just getting back." Groans all round. Mutterings of "Here we go again!" "God in heaven, does it never stop?" Someone suggested he ought to be gagged before he drove them all mad, and Gill, obligingly, clamped a hand over his mouth, but the hand was small and the voice was powerful, and Nicky, in any case, in a really determined fit of pique, was not one to be easily deflected.

"Twelve poxy weeks jarring your spine to fragments on every crummy, makeshift, potholed bit of ground that calls itself a stage between here and the Gulf of flaming Aqaba—" He took Gill's hand away from his mouth. "Can't even get on the poxy aeroplane and go home at the end of it."

"You could always," said a dry voice from the other side of the bench, "have stayed behind and gone to Manchester."

"I didn't want to go to Manchester— I've been to Manchester! Anyway—" he pulled Gill's hand into his lap—"I wasn't asked to go to Manchester."

"Well, just shut up moaning, then."

"Hm!"

Nicky subsided again in a hump. Gill ran a soothing hand through the tumbled curls. Manchester, indeed! Everybody knew that the half of the Company which had gone to Manchester were to all intents and purposes the second half. Not exactly inferior, but certainly not the cream. All the brightest of the up-and-coming talents —Zoë and Tanya, Derek of the dry voice, Nicky, Gill, István—they had all of them been sent off on the foreign tour. Whilst they in Tel Aviv and Haifa, in Ankara and Istanbul, had been dazzling audiences with virtuoso show pieces, the half that were left, with Alex and Andrea to give them backbone (for Alex and Andrea were nothing if not reliable) had been solidly ploughing their way through all the old war horses—*Sylphides* and *Giselle*, Rose Adagios and Sugar Plum Fairies, Act II of *Swan Lake*—to delight the citizens of Manchester, Macclesfield and all points north. It would, without any doubt, have been counted something of a failure to have been one of the ones to stay behind. At the same time—

"Five poxy days!" Nicky slumped on the bench, head on Gill's shoulder. "God's toenails!"

"I don't know about God's," said Tanya. "Mine certainly feel as if someone's been playing the xylophone on them with a couple of steam hammers."

"So who's surprised? After twelve weeks' slog—and how about that *last* abortion?" Nicky sat himself up again, twisting his head round to look over the back of the bench at Tanya. "Like trying to dance on a switchback . . . I swear to God that stage came up and hit me."

Derek said: "Serve you right." Someone else said it was a pity it didn't happen more often.

"Anyway," said Tanya, "it wasn't their fault. They can't help having earth tremors."

"Earth tremors!" Nicky threw back his head. "Earth tremors my eyeball! That wasn't any earth tremor, that was the stage. It's the way they build 'em. No idea, these Orientals."

Tanya wrinkled her forehead.

"*Are* Turks Orientals?" she said.

"Of course they are! What did you think they were? Mongols?"

"I thought someone said they were Muslims."

"So what's that got to do with it? They can still be Orientals, can't they?"

"I suppose so," said Tanya. "If you say so."

"Well, I do say so! And as for flaming *earth* tremors—"

"Yes, all right, all right! Don't go on about it!"

"I'm not going on about it. I just—"

"Just want me to take your word against theirs."

"Just want you to *admit* that earth tremors or no earth tremors—"

"Oh, for heaven's sake! Anything to keep you quiet . . . yes, yes, I admit it! I admit whatever you want me to admit! There! Does that satisfy you?" Tanya dropped a kiss on the end of his nose. "Earth tremors or no earth tremors . . . you have it your own way, my sweet. You usually do."

There could at least be no disputing that. His worst enemies would scarcely have denied Nicky his talent for winning over: either bludgeoned or beguiled, one capitulated in the end. It was not so much that he could have argued the hind leg off a donkey as that even at his most outrageous, his most preposterous, his most altogether infuriating, he was still endowed with a certain undeniable charm of manner, all the more persuasive for being if not precisely unconscious at any rate unassumed. Even Derek the dour found it impossible to remain out of humour with him for more than a few minutes at a stretch. Even Madame, behind her glacial ramparts, had now and again been observed to defrost by a couple of degrees. As for little Gill, with her beautiful deep-set eyes, black as coal in the pale, rather intense face, with her raven hair, smooth and straight and shining, classically pulled back from its centre parting—little Gill, who at the age of twenty looked like nothing so much as some inscrutable, thirteen-year-old madonna—she who ought by long exposure to have been immune was the most vulnerable of them all. Nicky, in Gill's book, could do no wrong. He was her beloved cousin, her adored partner, her knight in shining armour. Not a soul in the Company who wasn't aware of it— save perhaps Nicky himself.

He grinned now, provocatively, at Tanya over the back of the bench.

"If I'd known you were the sort of girl who gave in *that* easily—"

"Yes?" said Tanya.

Derek half turned in his seat.

"You can knock that off," he said, "right here and now."

"Oh?" The provocative grin instantly switched direction. "That wouldn't be an invitation, would it?"

"No, it would not! More in the nature of a none too friendly warning . . . you just keep your big beady eyes off other people's property."

Nicky pulled a face at him and collapsed again.

"If there's one thing I can't stand," he said, "it's possessive men." He settled his head back on to its resting place on Gill's shoulder, frowned, wriggled, sat up accusingly. "When are you going to get a bit of flesh on you, wench? Look at you! Like a skeleton . . . How can I rest my weary head on your ample bosom when you're all skin and bone?"

"If you didn't talk so damned much,"

said Derek, "you wouldn't have a weary head."

"No," said Tanya. "Neither would the rest of us."

With slow dignity, Nicky slid himself off the bench and on to the ground.

"I shall sleep," he said. "I am plainly not appreciated." He laid his head in Gill's lap. "If I fall into unwakeable slumber, just leave me here . . . it's perfectly obvious that no one would miss me."

"I would," said Gill.

She looked down at the curly head, and for a moment it was almost as if someone were walking over her grave. *She* would miss him so much it was terrifying even to think of—and yet, for all that, and all too frequently, it was something that she did think of. If one day Nicky were no longer to be there—if one day he were to die, or to go away, or to find someone else—what would she do? How would she manage? How would it be possible even to go on living, loving him as much as she did, so desperately?

There were some who might have wondered why she went on loving him at all, since it caused her so much anguish. The fact of the matter was, she couldn't help herself. She could no more have stopped loving Nicky than she could have stopped breathing. It came just as naturally to her: it was every bit as necessary. She had loved him too long to break free of the habit now. She always had loved him, right from the very earliest days, from even before the time when his father had run off to Venezuela with a red-headed lady from the tennis club and poor, weak, pretty Auntie Annabel had killed herself with an overdose of sleeping pills, leaving Nicky to fend for himself. She had known, naturally, that what had happened was all extremely shocking and the most terrible tragedy, she had known that Nicky had been the One to Discover the Body and that he must therefore be treated Extra Specially Nicely until the memory of it had faded, but yet it had been the most heavenly, glorious day of her life, the day on which

Nicky had come to live with them in Clapham, in the house overlooking the Common with Gill and her mother and grumbling old crosspatch of a Nanty. It had been Nicky himself who had christened her Nanty. Unable to make up his mind between "aunty" and "nan", he had settled on a compromise which had been promptly adopted as permanent. Nanty, of course, had been his willing slave from the moment he had first arrived on the doorstep, all blue eyes and black curls and engaging, gap-toothed grin, but not even Nanty had ever worshipped with quite the same intensity of passion as Gill. It wasn't only the curls and the grin, but the fact that he was a boy and four years her senior and could do wonderful, breathtaking things like hanging upside down from the branches of the apple tree, or walking on his hands the whole length of the lawn, or even, which quite turned her stomach, shinning up the drainpipe and playing leapfrog amongst the chimneypots. He had made her try it once and had taunted her for a yellow-belly when half way up she had suddenly become too paralyzed with fear to move in either direction, but then in the end he had relented and come to her rescue, as sooner or later he always did, because "You can't help it: you're only a girl."

She had humbly accepted it then: she humbly accepted it now. People thought that she was blind, but it wasn't that at all. She was perfectly well aware that Nicky had his faults. She knew him to have been spoilt, for her mother, in her anxiety to make him feel wanted, had tended to cosset, whilst Nanty had doted and still did. Even Alex, later on—and goodness knows Alex had had problems enough of his own to cope with—had not been wholly impervious; even he, more often than not, had been coaxed into "making allowances". Only Gill herself, with a stubbornness and a strength of will quite equal to Nicky's own, even despite her adulation, had ever stood firm or sought to oppose—and then nine times out of ten had been over-ridden by Nanty or reasoned with by Alex. All things considered, the wonder of it was not that Nicky *could* be selfish, but that he was not more frequently so. The rest of the Company, she knew, found him erratic, irrational, over-emotional—someone in her hearing had once described him as "wilfully capricious". So perhaps he was, but what possible difference could it make? For all his weaknesses she loved him just as dearly, just as uncritically, as she had ever done. If he in turn loved her with a carelessness that seemed but lukewarm by comparison, what right had she to complain? Nicky had not asked for her devotion. She had bestowed it on him of her own free will: it was for him to do with as he wished. If at the end of the day he should choose to discard it, she would have no one to blame but herself.

They took off at last, forty-five minutes behind schedule. She didn't have to wake Nicky, because he wasn't asleep. He never did sleep when there was the least possibility of anything happening. Others might nod off—Nicky, like an animal, remained for ever on the alert, ear cocked for the slightest sound. By the time they arrived at Heathrow, three hours later, he was in high good humour and back once again on top of the world. They shared a cab into town with Derek and Tanya, whose one idea was to reach home as quickly as possible and spend the rest of the evening doing "absolutely nothing".

"Preferably," said Derek, "in bed."

"In bed?" Nicky seemed quite shocked. "Doing nothing?"

"*Absolutely* nothing."

"Nothing at *all?*"

"Nothing," said Derek, "at all. It is quite possible, you know—strange though it may seem to you."

"Well, for crying out loud!" Nicky sat back in disgust. "How mind-shatteringly boring."

"What's so boring about it? Don't you ever do nothing?"

"Not if I can possibly avoid it."

Derek shook his head. He turned reprovingly to Gill.

"You haven't got this chap trained

right. You'll have to explain some time . . . there is nothing in the least bit *boring* about doing nothing."

"Always depending, of course," said Tanya, "on who you do it with. You obviously couldn't spend an evening doing it with just anybody. On the other hand—" she chucked Nicky under the chin—"if you only take the trouble to choose the right person—"

"All the more reason," he said, promptly, "for doing something positive. What's the point of taking the trouble to choose the right person and then not doing anything with them? Might just as well climb into bed with a chastity belt and a good book—might just as well be dead, if it comes to that."

"Lord, Lord!" said Derek. "Doesn't he ever let up, even for just five minutes? Doesn't he *ever* just lie back and relax?"

Gill smiled; one of her rare, sunny smiles.

"Not very often," she said.

"Well, God only knows how you manage to live with him."

Certainly Nicky wasn't the most comfortable of persons to live with—but then, he never had been. If it was a comfortable life she was after, she would not have moved in with him in the first place. She had known well enough what she was letting herself in for. *Dolce far niente* played no part in Nicky's make-up. There could never be any "sweet doing nothing" with him around: never any question of just lying back and relaxing. It was ceaseless activity from the moment he woke up in the morning till the moment he climbed into bed at night— and that, all too often, was not until the small hours. More than once, these past months, she had been woken by the sound of his key in the latch at two or even three in the morning. More than once she had lain there, listening, as the water ran in the bathroom, the footsteps padded along the corridor, the door of Nicky's bedroom opened and then closed. More than once she had kept herself awake right round till morning, fruitlessly wondering where he had been, what he had been doing—whom he had been doing it with. Sometimes, over a snatched breakfast of black coffee and toast, he would volunteer some snippet of information—would say that he'd been "round with friends", that he'd "gone to a party", "discovered a new club". Other times he wouldn't say anything at all. She never asked him outright, nor pressed for any details. She knew that she mustn't, or he would grow impatient, he would grow tired of her, he would feel that she was intruding. Whatever she did, she would never nag at him, nor push herself in where she might not be wanted. It was no business of hers how Nicky chose to spend his spare time: he had not asked her to move in with him. The only hope she could have was that one day—one day, perhaps, he would notice that she was there and would decide that he might do worse than to settle for her. Until then she would remain in the background, do her best not to obtrude; strive, above all, to conquer those twisting torments of jealousy that racked her every time she pictured Nicky with another girl. No sense in deluding herself: there had to be others. She knew that. Apart from anything else, she had seen the effect that he had on women—older women, mostly, but younger ones as well. So long as none of them ever succeeded in capturing his affections, that was as much as she asked. She could stand the thought of his sleeping with them: it was the thought of his falling in love which caused her heart to stand still. If *that* should ever happen—

They dropped Derek and Tanya off in Notting Hill Gate ("We won't ask you in," said Derek, "because quite frankly I don't think I could take it") and went on in the cab to Guilford Street, to the flat which for the past year they had been sharing and where for two years before that Nicky had lived with a friend called Vic who had been in catering and now had his own restaurant. The flat was smallish but self-contained, on the topmost floor of a tall, narrow house with area steps going down to the basement and a fanlight over the front door. The first, second and ground floors were offices of various kinds, solicitors and quantity surveyors and rather seedy theatrical agents, while down in the basement was Manuela, the fat Spanish housekeeper who had adopted Nicky as her *angelito* and would cheerfully, had he only cared to take advantage, have devoted every minute of her spare time, and most likely every penny of her earnings, administering to his welfare. (He was, fortunately, not that unscrupulous, but still it was Gill who had been the one to remind him about bringing back a present.)

Five minutes away from the flat was the British Museum—useful enough as a landmark and for pointing out to foreigners, though not, in truth, a place that either of them was much in the habit of visiting. Gill had been taken a couple of times, in a party from ballet school, and Nicky had once spent half an hour in there sheltering from the rain, but really, on the whole, it had to be said, it was a building they knew far better from the outside than the in. A short step further on, a brisk ten-minute walk of a morning, down Southampton Row, along Kingsway, round the curve of the Aldwych, and there was the theatre. It had been the ostensible reason for Gill's move. The daily journey from Clapham was becoming too much of a drag. It was true that Alex was there to take her in in the mornings and almost always took her home again at night, but she didn't want to have to rely on Alex for transport. Far more convenient to be within walking distance, and since Nicky had a room going begging—Nicky, after some initial hesitation, had agreed that it might be quite a good idea. Alex hadn't seemed so certain, but that was only because Alex had grown too accustomed to stand *in loco parentis* and still regarded her in the light of a little girl. He couldn't really have any worries: not when she was with Nicky.

She suggested, as they toiled up the three steep flights of uncarpeted stairs to the flat, that they might call round on Alex that evening "to see how the frozen north had been".

"Yeah—" Nicky threw open the front door and humped their suitcases through to the hall. "Could do, I suppose."

He didn't sound any too enthusiastic at the prospect. She hastened to reassure him.

"We don't *have* to. We could always go tomorrow. It was just if you didn't happen to have anything else on—"

"Well, to tell the truth," he said, "I had thought of popping out to Chalk Farm and looking in on Vic and Trudi."

"Oh—"

She waited, hopefully, to see whether he might suggest they both popped out to Chalk Farm to look in on Vic and Trudi. That could surely not come into the category of pushing herself in where she wasn't wanted? He could surely not object to her going with him to see Vic and Trudi? They were two of the few, the very, very few, of Nicky's friends whom she had ever been allowed to meet. He

you. You needn't think *I* haven't suggested it, because I have. Times without number. He talks about you, all right—my God, how he talks! The hours we've spent . . . I tell you, the things I don't know about you and Alex would fit on the back of a postage stamp. But as for actually letting me *meet* you—"

Alex used to try explaining it by saying that both the family and the ballet were so all-embracing as to be smothering—that it wasn't very surprising if Nicky should feel the need to break out, to keep a part of himself separate.

"You can't chain him down, Gilly. You've got to let him go his own way."

She knew that. She accepted it now as she never could have done as a child. She just wished that Nicky's way, whatever it was, might also be hers. Wherever it was leading him, she wanted to be there at his side. And surely it hadn't done any harm, introducing her to Vic? It hadn't intruded in any way on his precious privacy. When Vic had still been sharing the flat with him, she had never gone round there without ringing first to check that she would be welcome. When he had moved out to Chalk Farm, to fulfil his long-cherished dream of opening a restaurant, she had never once fished for an invitation, but had waited patiently until Nicky of his own accord—or was it, perhaps, by Vic's prompting?—had decided one evening to take her along, and then, as far as she could see, she hadn't spoilt anyone's fun. They'd stayed on, afterwards, when the place had closed, going upstairs to the flat above the restaurant where Vic lived in careless rapture with Trudi, his large, jolly, middle-aged girl friend who came from Bavaria and looked after the till, and it had seemed to her that they had all got on well enough together. Trudi had become rather drunk and giggly, and Nicky had encouraged her, as Nicky was wont to do, and had flirted quite outrageously (as he was also wont to do) with one eye on Vic to see how he was taking it, but Vic obviously wasn't one of his possessive men for he'd just grinned and shaken his big shaggy head

and solemnly advised Gill to "watch that
lad, if I were you, when he gets you back
home . . ."

Surely it wouldn't hurt him, now, to
take her with him? She waited, but all he
said was:

"Why don't *you* drop round?"

"On Alex? By myself?"

"Why not? He'd far rather see you than
me."

She looked at him, reproachfully.

"You know that's not true. He'd rather
see both of us."

"Go on, you were always his favourite!
Spoilt you rotten."

"Spoilt *me?*" she said. "I like that! You
were the one that used to get away with
all the murder."

"Ah, but not with Alexis . . . no flies
on that boyo. He had me sussed out right
from the beginning. I've had enough
strips torn off me in my time."

Gill fell silent, watching as Nicky went
through to his own bedroom, dumped his
case on the bed and began in his usual
haphazard fashion on the process of

unpacking. She watched him stuffing shirts, socks, sweaters, pants, all at random into the same drawer. She supposed that some time she would be weak enough to go in there after him and put it all to rights—not, to be fair to Nicky, that he expected it of her. He was perfectly happy to live in a muddle, he had never demanded that she be his slave.

"Nanty will be disappointed," she said.

"Yes—" He straightened up, swinging a pair of limp grey practice shoes by their frayed elastic. He seemed, for a moment, genuinely concerned. "Yes, I suppose she will . . . Tell her—" he lobbed the shoes into a corner, together with a plastic bag full of old tights and dirty sweat shirts— "tell her I had to go somewhere. Say I'll be round in the week. Tomorrow, or Friday, or some time. Perhaps we'll go and have lunch with the old love. How about that?" He picked up his sponge bag. "I'm going to have a shower. What time are you leaving?"

"Oh—" She shrugged a shoulder. "I might as well go straight away."

"Not going to change?"

"What for?" *She* was perfectly respectable: she hadn't travelled back in a navy blue seaman's sweater three sizes too large and a pair of old Levis with frayed bottoms and a zip held together with a safety pin. She spared herself a cursory glance in the long hall mirror filched from home. She was presentable enough. "It's only Alex," she said.

Nicky raised a quizzical eyebrow.

"Poor old Alexis! You mean that's all he rates?"

"No, of course not!" She was quick to refute the suggestion. "Of course I didn't mean that. I didn't mean that at all. I just meant—" She stopped. What had she just meant? Not that Alex wasn't *worth* the trouble of changing for. Certainly not that. Only, perhaps, that with Alex there wasn't any need to impress. With him one could relax and be oneself and not care too much if now and again one wasn't always quite looking at one's best. Alex, after all, was family—or at any rate, as good as. (But then, she thought, so was

Nicky—and with him it wasn't even "as good as". On the other hand, Nicky had never stood *in loco parentis*. Perhaps that was what it was.) "All I meant," she said, "was that one doesn't have to doll oneself up."

"Hm . . . well, in that case—" he gave her cheek a pinch as he passed her on his way to the bathroom—"how about making us a quick cup of coffee before you go?"

2

"HELLO! Anyone at home?"

Gill stood for a moment, front door flung open, key still in the lock, smelling the familiar smell of old building, dank and musty, almost church-like. The long passage, high and narrow, with its ancient strip of red carpet, its dark walls crowding in, stretched away before her to the kitchen at the far end, to the stairs that led down to the basement and up, the other way, to the attics.

The house overlooking the Common was nothing very special—terraced Victorian, red-brick, single-fronted, four storeys high if you included both the attics and the basement, three and a bit if you forgot about the attics but included the two rooms on the half landing at the turn of the stairs.

It had, without doubt, seen better days,

and could hardly have been an object of architectural splendour even then.

The most prominent features of its decoration were the rows of glazed tiles, spinach-green and chocolate, with the stained-glass lilies above the front door and the weather-beaten lions, two eroded stone sentinels, at the foot of the crumbling steps. It was nothing very special, save that it was home. It had been home as far back as memory stretched: it would go on being home all the time that Alex was still there—Alex and Nanty both, but Alex in particular. Home could never be home without Alex.

She still remembered, in vivid detail, the day he had first come to the house, awkward and ill at ease in his dreadful, lumpy sweater and his patched grey trousers that had quite obviously been cut down for him. The sweater had needed mending at the elbows and the trousers had come out at the knees, and his toes, when without being asked he had removed his big clumsy boots to avoid tramping mud down the hallway, had poked out through the holes in his neon yellow socks. As toes went, they had looked none too clean, and his blond hair, straggling and unkempt, had been so badly in need of a wash that it more nearly resembled dark mouse than blond. He had been sprung upon them without warning—brought back by Gill's mother for "tea". Gill's mother, despite having been widowed at an early age and finding life a struggle, had been of a somewhat more robust nature than poor, pretty, feather-brained Aunt Annabel. Instead of going under she had turned her hand to teaching, spending five afternoons a week giving mime and movement classes at an East London comprehensive, and five mornings and most of her evenings giving private ballet classes down in the basement, which had been specially converted for the purpose into a studio.

She had long been in the habit of bringing the more promising of her comprehensive pupils back home with her for tea, but never before had she brought such a one as this. Gill and Nicky had sat silently staring at him across the table, watching the way that he ate, with his mouth wide open and his elbows all splayed out, wielding his knife and fork like pickaxes and clutching at his mug of tea with both hands as if there were no such thing as a handle. They had been most put out when they had heard that from now on Alex would be coming to tea twice a week and staying on afterwards to take classes with them. Why should they have to share their precious private lesson time with a strange uncouth boy who ate with his mouth open and walked about in rags? *They* weren't allowed to eat with their mouths open: why should they have to suffer him? They had been even more put out when three months later, without any prior consultation, Mrs. Conway had suddenly announced over the breakfast table one morning that she had successfully applied to become a foster mother and that the strange uncouth boy, who, they had discovered, had no parents of his own and lived in a local children's home, was coming to take up permanent residence with them. Their resentment and horror had known no bounds. They had grown grudgingly accustomed, by now, to have Alex share their classes with them, they didn't mind that so much—indeed, if anything, they rather enjoyed it, because it gave them a chance to prove their superiority and to show off; but as to having him *live* with them—

Nicky in particular had been resentful —more than resentful, he had been bitterly jealous. For all his rags and tatters and appalling table manners, Alex at the age of thirteen had been three years Nicky's senior and as such had represented not only a challenge but also a very real threat to his own hard-won and still somewhat precarious security. He had been an intruder, a usurper, a would-be ouster of affections, and Nicky from the word go had been bent on making his life a misery. Left to herself, Gill would in all probability have been open-minded, for she bore the stranger no special ill will; as it was, she had taken her cue from Nicky. Even today it brought a blush of shame to her cheeks, when she looked back at the way they had treated him—jeering at his freckles and his blond hair (which Nicky had arbitrarily adjudged, for a boy, to be "cissy"), poking fun at the way he spoke, mimicking his dropped Hs, mocking at his bad grammar, doing everything they could think of to make him feel inferior —and all, like the cowards that they were, well out of sight or sound of her mother or of Nanty. Alex had taken it in stoical silence, as if by virtue of their better fortune in life they had every right to lord it over him and sneer. Sometimes, when they crudely imitated his accent, he would grow very red and would bite his lip and clench his fists, and then they would exult, because then they knew they had succeeded in discomfiting him, and if they could only discomfit him often enough and long enough they might even succeed, in the end, into actually goading him into running away. What had been funniest of all and given them the greatest cause for mirth was when he conscientiously strove to speak as they did, trying to imitate *their* accents, because theirs were "posh" and his was "common". That was the finest opportunity of the lot when it came to discomfiting. Then they really *did* make him squirm. And yet, despite it all, he had persevered. They never had succeeded in goading him to breaking point. After a time, they had simply stopped trying.

It was Gill who had been the first to capitulate. She hadn't wanted to, for it made her feel disloyal to Nicky, still gallantly continuing the campaign, but not even for Nicky's sake could she have gone on being nasty to Alex. He was too patient, too gentle, too altogether good-natured—and even after all their hatefulness he had borne no grudges. Nicky would never have picked her up, as Alex did, and cuddled her when she fell out of a tree and hurt herself: Nicky would never have taken her on his knee and petted her, nor wiped away her tears with the sleeve of his shirt. With Nicky it was always "Don't be such a cry baby" or

"Serve you right for being clumsy." To be kissed and cosseted was quite a new experience: she had responded in spite of herself. One day, her sense of justice outraged, she had even gone so far as to leap to the defence of the intruder at the expense of her adored Nicky. It was when Alex had been with them for about six months. They had gone out into the garden to play cricket, all three of them together, and a dispute had arisen as to whether Gill, being (a) only a girl and (b) only a very *small* girl, should be granted the concession of being bowled at underarm. Alex had maintained that she should, while Nicky had said that either she played properly or she didn't play at all, and that in his opinion it would probably be a good thing if she didn't play at all, since she couldn't catch for toffee and was nothing but a stupid nuisance anyway. Somehow or other, it had escalated rapidly into a vicious slanging match —vicious, that is, on Nicky's side. Gill, carelessly swinging herself to and fro on the swing which Alex had fashioned for her with a piece of orange box and two lengths of rope attached to the branches of that very same apple tree up which Nicky was accustomed to swarm, had suddenly heard him shout:

"Anyway, *you* can't say anything, *you* don't even know who your father was . . . *you*'re nothing but a bastard!"

A silence had settled on the garden. Gill, aware of tension, had stopped swinging and looked across the lawn to where the two boys stood facing each other, Nicky, his curls all in a tangle, still clutching the cricket bat and ball, Alex frozen in the act of placing the bails on top of the stumps. She wondered what the significance of the word bastard was, and why Nicky had spat it out with such malicious triumph: *YOU don't even know who your father was . . . YOU're nothing but a bastard!* She could only conclude that it was something to do with the fact that Alex, unlike other people, had never seemed to have any father, and while that was admittedly a bit odd and she didn't quite see how it could have happened, it certainly could in no way have been his fault and it certainly wasn't fair for Nicky to be taunting him with it. He had turned quite pale beneath his freckles. She had never known one of their jibes have such obvious and shattering effect before. Even when they had mocked at him for his attempts to better himself he had borne it with fortitude and stiff upper lip. Now his upper lip was covered in perspiration and his lower one was trembling. They had been trying all along to hit upon something that would really hurt—something that would really cut to the quick, really dig a knife into the heart. At last they had succeeded—and she didn't like it one little bit. It gave her no satisfaction to see Alex standing there trembling. If anyone were to be made to suffer knives in the heart, then let it be Nicky, not Alex. Alex had already, it seemed to her, endured more than his share of the world's unkindnesses.

With cool deliberation, Gill had slipped off her swing. Walking across to the rockery, where next door's cat was sunning itself athwart a clump of heather, she had said casually:

"At least if Alex *had* had a father, I don't expect he'd have gone running off and left him."

She had known she was treading forbidden ground, for she had been warned often enough by both her mother and Nanty, but still the violence of Nicky's reaction had taken her by surprise. He had come at her, face contorted, with the cricket bat: it was only Alex, managing just in time to snatch at his arm, who had saved her. The next second, and Nicky in his fury had turned on Alex himself. Alex was taller than Nicky by a good few inches, and wirier, too, but still he had been hard put to it to defend himself against the savage onslaught. Nicky, panting and sobbing, with tears of rage and mortification rolling down his cheeks, had been dragged away at last by an outraged Nanty, who had seemed to take it for granted that the entire incident had been Alex's fault. She had berated him soundly for having "upset the poor mite".

"A big lad of your age—in your position, too. Ought to be ashamed of yourself."

When Gill had tried to protest, Alex had stopped her. He had told her later that she "mustn't never say nothing like that" to Nicky again because it was "very hurtful—specially coming from you". She had been quite indignant at that.

"Well, but it was him that started it . . . *he* was hurtful to *you*."

Alex had said that that was different: that that didn't matter because "he could take it". Implying, she had had to assume, that Nicky couldn't, which had always struck her as being rather paradoxical, since it was Nicky, not Alex, who was the one to be for ever getting himself into scrapes, coming to blows, spoiling for a fight—not that he ever tried fighting with Alex again. From that day on, possibly because Alex had kept silent and allowed all the blame to be heaped on his own shoulders, Nicky's attitude had altered. There had been no more laughing and jeering, no more cheap gibes. Affection had followed swiftly upon the heels of respect. Before the year was out, Alex had become one of the family. When Gill's mother had died, but four short years later, Alex had been the one to whom they had all, instinctively, turned for support. He had not failed them. It had been Alex who had comforted Gill, who had consoled Nanty, who had kept Nicky on the rails: Alex who had assumed all responsibility and borne henceforth all burdens: Alex, even now, who stayed at home in the old house overlooking the Common so that Nanty should not feel herself deserted, so that Gill and Nicky should always have somewhere to come back to. Without Alex to take care of them, they would all have been lost.

He appeared now at the far end of the passage, wrapping a bath towel round himself.

"Hi, there—"

"Alex!"

Joyfully, she slammed the front door

behind her and went racing pell mell down the passage towards him. He stood waiting for her, arms outstretched, just as he had always used to do in the days when she was still a little girl and needed cuddling.

"Hello, sweetheart! How goes it? Had a good trip?"

"Fabulous! How about you?"

"Well, at least it was quiet," he said. "I imagine that's more than can be claimed for your little excursion . . . I'll bet they're still reeling from the shock out there. The thought of Nicky let loose on foreign shores without me to keep an eye on him is one that quite makes the blood run cold. I've been expecting headlines in the paper any day . . . *BRITISH BALLET DANCER STARTS THIRD WORLD WAR* . . . I suppose you haven't left him behind in some Turkish gaol, have you?"

"No! Of course I haven't!" She laughed, and hugged him. "Don't be so silly . . . as if I would!"

"Where is he, then? Up to no good, I'll be bound."

"He had to go and see someone. He said he'd be round later in the week. We thought we might both come round and have lunch with Nanty." She paused. "How—er—is Nanty?"

"Well—" Alex readjusted his bath towel. "Let's say she was still alive and kicking when I got back . . . Do you want to pop up and say hello to her while I finish my bath? I'll take you out for a meal, if you like—or have you already eaten?"

"No, just picked at bits and pieces. I'm starving."

"Go on, then—" He gave her a little push towards the stairs. "Go and do your duty and get it over with, and maybe I'll let you pick your own restaurant."

Gill pulled a face.

"All right—if I must."

"You know you must. There'll be all hell let loose if she finds out you're back and I haven't sent you up to see her. She'll only accuse me of keeping you from

45

her. God knows, I'm already in her bad books . . . I don't want to do anything to make it worse!"

Nanty had her own rooms at the top of the house. She had moved up there when Nicky left home, declaring that the family was breaking up and that she wasn't one as needed telling when her usefulness was over: *she* knew when she wasn't wanted. No amount of reasoned talk could persuade her out of it. She had been up there ever since, living hermitlike in stubborn solitude, cooking her own meals on two ancient gas rings, splashing the walls with grease, emptying her slops out of the window on to the flower beds far below sooner than walk a few yards along the passage to the bathroom at the other end. There was nothing very much that either Alex or Gill could do to alter the situation. Nicky might have coaxed her out of it if he would, but Nicky only said let the old dear alone, she was perfectly happy pottering about in her squalor. He was probably quite right, and anyway it was not as if she were completely by herself. She had a moulting canary bird in a cage and a ginger tom cat of disreputable appearance and incredible vintage who occasionally misbehaved himself in awkward places on the stairs.

Today the old lady was in one of her aggressive moods, complaining angrily about Alex, who had "gone away and left her here in this great mausoleum of a place at the mercy of every gangster in London," but that it was "all you could expect from a charity boy who'd been dragged out of a home."

"No gratitude, no gratitude anywhere. I don't know why she bothered with him. I told her so at the time. I said, you'll regret it, you see if you don't . . . Now he's threatening to put the cat down the lavatory and pull the chain on it."

"Nanty, how can you?" said Gill. "You know Alex would never do anything of the kind. And as for leaving you here—" How many times had he begged her to let him make arrangements for her to be looked after while he was away? And how many times had she furiously accused him of wanting to "get rid of her"? It was all so terribly unfair. Why pick on poor Alex? He had already done more for her than she had any right to expect, cross old witch. At the back of her mind, of course, she still had the lingering memory of that day on the lawn when she had rescued her favourite from his bullying clutches. She had never forgiven him for that. But as for still casting up at him that he had been "dragged out of a home"— Alex, who had fought so hard, had pulled himself up from nothing to become one of the best-loved and certainly one of the most respected of dancers the New London had ever had—

Even making all allowances for old age and blind prejudice, Gill could not stand there and listen to torrents of abuse poured out against Alex. She stayed only five minutes then made her escape, glad in any case to be out of the pungent pall of stale stew and tom cat. She decided that if Nicky wanted to run the risk of eating lunch up there, he might: she was certainly having no part in it.

Down in the more wholesome atmosphere of the ground floor she found Alex just emerging from the bathroom.

"That was quick," he said.

"Yes." She wrinkled her nose. "It's One of her Days. She thinks you're out to murder the cat."

"Oh, so that's what it is! I wondered what I'd done."

"Did you actually do *anything*?"

"Yes, I took the wretched creature down to the vet the first night I got back . . . poor bloody animal's losing all its fur."

"Well, it must be at least a hundred and fifty. It's probably just normal baldness."

She followed him through into his bedroom, perching herself matter of factly on the edge of the dressing-table to continue the conversation as he dressed. Alex, with equal matter of factness, flung his dressing-gown over the back of a chair and took a clean shirt from out of the wardrobe. There had once been a time, when he first came to live with them, when Gill's presence would have embarrassed him acutely: there had once been a time, a few years later, when Gill herself would have been embarrassed acutely. She often thought that if it had not been for Nicky, both she and Alex might have grown up to be quite inhibited. Fortunately, with him for ever dashing about the place stark naked, they had never stood much chance. It really wasn't possible for anyone to remain shy for long with Nicky around.

"So how's the new girl?" she said.

"New girl?"

"The one from the Etoile."

"Oh, Danielle . . . Danielle Dupont. Of course, you haven't seen her, have you? I keep forgetting. People stop seeming new when you've been on tour with them for three months."

"So what's she like?"

"Mm—" He stood a moment, considering a tie. "Much as you might expect . . . very French, very come hitherish . . . I suppose I'd better put this damn thing on, just in case. Depends where you want to go."

She thought for a moment of suggesting they drive out to Chalk Farm to eat at Vic and Trudi's. He wouldn't need a tie at Vic and Trudi's, it was all very informal. But then, perhaps, Nicky mightn't like it if they suddenly turned up without being asked. He might think they were spying on him.

"I don't mind," she said. "Anywhere will do. What's she like as a dancer?"

"As a dancer—" He had already put the tie round his neck in spite of what she had said. She wondered why he bothered, when she knew how much he disliked them. There was really no need for him to go dressing himself up just for her. "As a dancer . . . well, she's got lots of sparkle, lots of verve. Good technique, not much depth . . . it's all very pyrotechnical. And talking of pyrotechnics—" He glanced at his watch. "I must just dash and make a quick telephone call before we leave."

She looked up at him with quick concern.

"You weren't already going somewhere?"

"Nowhere special—I can easily duck out. I said there was a chance I might, if you or Nicky dropped round. You stay there and twiddle your thumbs, it won't take me five seconds."

Maybe not—but for all that he obviously didn't want her there while he was doing it. She wondered who it was that he was putting off. It made her feel guilty to think of Alex foregoing pleasures of his own simply in order to take her out to dinner. It was about time he left her and Nicky to get on with it and started concentrating a bit more on himself.

She walked across to the window, pressing her nose against the pane and staring out into the garden, still a-bloom with late summer roses. She and Nicky had never lifted a finger to do anything out there. It was Alex who had kept the encroaching brambles at bay and periodically shorn the grass to respectable length. Not that he cared for gardening any more than they, it was just that being Alex he couldn't bear to see it revert to untended jungle—and anyway, he had green fingers. He had but to dig a hole and toss in a packet of seeds, and lo and behold the seeds would grow, even if he had dug the hole at quite the wrong time of year or in quite the wrong part of the garden. In the middle of the lawn was the bird table he had made, and there on the apple tree, even now, hung the old rope swing. She wondered if he were keeping it for his own children to swing on—if he ever had any children of his own. At the rate he was going, he never would, cancelling engagements every time either she or Nicky chose to turn up on the spur of the moment. Of course, from a purely selfish point of view she would be only too glad if he didn't, for Alex with a wife and family would without any doubt be far less accessible than Alex all by himself; on the other hand, from *Alex*'s point of view—If he would only find someone pleasant and inoffensive, like funny old Kath, who had had a schoolgirl crush on him for donkey's years, or even Andrea, whom he'd been partnering for the last five—though perhaps upon reflection poor old Andy was getting a bit past it, she must be well into her thirties by now. But at least if he would just find *some*body. All this sleeping around couldn't be good for anyone, and least of all for Alex. Alex simply wasn't a sleeping around sort of person, he was a settling-down-having-a-family sort of person. She refused to believe that it could really make him happy, all this constant chopping and changing.

His telephone call took him considerably longer than the five seconds he had promised. She thought how the person at the other end, whoever it was (someone in the Company?) must be hating and resenting her. She, most certainly, would resent anyone who turned up and took Nicky away from her at the last minute. Alex, however, did not have the air of one who had been given a rough time. He drove her into town, to a "little place" in Soho. It was far more expensive than she had bargained for, but when she remonstrated with him he only told her to mind her own business and get on and eat something.

"You look as if you could do with a good square meal inside you. What's the matter with that boy? Doesn't he feed you properly?"

She laughed.

"He hardly ever feeds him*self*—doesn't have time to stop for anything so mundane as food."

Besides, the thought of Nicky bothering to feed her—

"Hm." Alex toyed a moment with the menu. "So how did he behave himself in foreign parts?"

She was puzzled to think what he could mean by "how did he behave himself?" How did he expect that Nicky should behave himself? It was admittedly the first time they had ever been on tour abroad without Alex, but what on that account did he anticipate happening?

"No problems?" said Alex. "Didn't cause any riots or get himself arrested or—"

"Or what?" she said. "He was as good as gold." Once or twice he had done one of his famous disappearing acts, so that everyone had rushed about in a state of panic saying "Where's Nicky? What's happened to Nicky?" but he'd always turned up again in the end. He always did turn up again, sooner or later. You'd think they'd have learnt by now. Nicky wasn't anywhere near as irresponsible as people seemed to imagine. To change the subject, she said: "Tell me about the plans for next season . . . there's a rumour going the rounds that Madame's had a brainstorm and is planning to revive that Adam thing."

"*Adam in the Garden of Eden*."

"Yes." She stared at him across the table. "You don't mean that she actually *is?* Not *Madame?* Actually going to chance her arm for once in her life?"

"Oh, come on, now, she's not such a

stick in the mud as all that! She did do the first production."

"Yes, and pretty quickly took it off again!"

"Well, be fair—at least she was prepared to give it a trial run. That's more than most others would have done at that time. Nine years ago, you know, the climate wasn't like it is now. It was a daring enough venture by anyone's standards."

And, certainly, the New London have never been noted for their daring. Impeccable good taste was their hallmark. They were not a company readily identified with the modern, the outré, the in any way experimental—and yet, almost a decade ago, they had risked a work that had unleashed such a storm of controversy as had not been enjoyed in ballet circles for many a long year. The storm had even spread beyond the high-walled enclosure of the ballet to the big wide world outside. A certain daily newspaper had shrilly demanded to know whether this is Art or whether it is Filth? Another newspaper had called for an X certificate. Still another had queried the moral rightness of encouraging little girls in pink tutus to go on learning how to point their toes and turn in circles if *this* was where it was going to lead them . . .

The controversy amongst purists had centred entirely upon the balletic validity of the piece. It was exciting, it was new, it called for no small degree of technical virtuosity, but that did not make it a ballet—or did it? Opinions then had been sharply divided, opinions today would probably still be so. As for the pure in heart, they had cared not whether it was a ballet or whether it was not a ballet: it had been the moral content which had preoccupied them.

"You probably wouldn't remember it too well," said Alex. "In any case, you were far too young to understand it."

"No, I wasn't," she said. "I read the programme notes. I remember it quite vividly . . . there was a snaky women in a red leotard and a man in what looked like nothing at all."

"That," said Alex, "was what all the fuss was about. The Fall of Adam Graphically Depicted . . . it was just a bit too graphic for its time. All right for the trendies, but far too explicit for the general public."

"Was it actually any good?"

"We happened to think so."

"I bet you were mad when it was withdrawn before you could have a shot at it!"

He shrugged.

"That's the way it goes."

"But after learning it and everything . . . she might at least have kept it on for another couple of performances."

"I don't think Heinz wanted her to. The version you saw was obviously the unexpurgated one—hence the impact it made on your lascivious schoolgirl mind. She insisted after that that he made some cuts. He was never too happy about it."

"I suppose she's going to keep them in?"

"Not if I have anything to do with it.

I've already warned her I don't believe in massacring other people's work when they're no longer around to defend themselves. Poor old Heinz would turn in his grave."

"Never tell me," said Gill, "that she's actually letting you have some say in the matter?"

He grinned.

"She hasn't got much option—she needs my services. I'm the only person left who still remembers it in any detail."

"Were you the one who talked her into it?"

"No, grant her that much, she thought of it herself. She said she wanted a vehicle."

"Vehicle? What sort of vehicle?"

"For bright new talent . . . here." He thrust a menu at her. "Take this and concentrate. What do you feel like eating?"

"Oh—steak—anything. Whatever you're having. I take it you will be dancing Adam?"

"Me?" He raised a quizzical eyebrow.

"I'm hardly bright new talent, would you say?"

"But Alex, you must! She couldn't not let you—it wouldn't be fair! Not after last time—"

"Last time," he gently reminded her, "was nine long years ago. What one is capable of at eighteen one is not necessarily capable of at twenty-seven."

"Oh, but that's rubbish! You're *more* capable now than you were then. Then you were only a gauche youth. Now—"

"Now?" he said. There was just the hint of a twinkle in his eye.

"Well, now you're—you're in the prime of your manhood!"

"Thank you," he said, gravely. "I shall endeavour to remember that next time I wake in the morning with a crick in my neck and an ache in my back and several pulled thigh muscles. It will be a great comfort to me."

"Oh, Alex! Be serious . . . you would *like* to dance Adam, wouldn't you?"

"I don't know—I'm not so sure that I would. It's hardly my scene, is it?

61

Cavorting about in the next to nothing performing prodigies of sexual gymnastics before an audience of admiring matrons . . . I think on the whole I'd rather leave it to the natural exhibitionists like Nicky. Got more hairs on his chest than I have —give 'em no end of a thrill! *And* he'd enjoy it while he was about it."

No denying the fact, Nicky would be in his element—but she refused to believe that Alex really and truly didn't care whether he danced the part or not. He was plainly enthusiastic about the ballet as a whole, and she trusted his judgement sufficiently to accept that if he said a work was worth while, then worth while it certainly was. The trouble with Alex was that when it came to judging him*self* he was too unassuming. That was the very reason he tended to get passed over—the very reason he made such an excellent partner but was so rarely allowed any of the limelight. All the same, if Nicky *were* to be lucky enough to land the name part—

"What about the snake woman?" she

said. "I suppose Andrea's got her eye on that?"

"*Andrea?* Have a heart! You surely don't see her in a red leotard playing the temptress?"

"Well, this Danielle creature, then."

"No." He shook his head. "Not subtle enough. Far too voluptuous . . . I'm going for the steak. That do you?"

"Yes, yes! Anything!" She would have eaten fried rhinoceros and chips had that been what he suggested. There were more important matters to worry about at this moment than what to eat for dinner. She thrust the menu back at him. "So what do you think?"

"About the steak?"

"No! The part!"

"Oh . . . the part!" This time there quite definitely *was* a twinkle in his eye. "Well . . . let's put it this way: it can't do any harm to keep your fingers crossed, can it? You just never know what your luck might be . . ."

It was midnight when Alex dropped her off again at Guilford Street. Nicky was not yet back. She sat up as long as she could, eager to tell him about the new production, and how, just possibly, if they kept their fingers crossed . . . but at some stage sleep must have overcome her, for the next thing she knew it was almost three o'clock in the morning and she slipping sideways off the sofa on to the floor. She glanced in, without much hope, on Nicky's room, just in case he had come back without her hearing, but there was still no sign of him. It was obviously going to be one of those nights. She reminded herself firmly, as she had had to remind herself so many times before, that Nicky had not asked her to move in and live with him—and he always did come back again in the end. The news would just have to wait until breakfast.

The news, as it happened, had to wait until long after breakfast: it was almost lunch time before she heard the sound of Nicky's key in the lock. He always did come back in the end—but how was it humanly possible not to feel anxious? How was it possible not to burst into tears of relief at the very sight of him? Nicky himself seemed surprised and almost indignant.

"You surely weren't *worried?*" he said. "For heaven's sake, you stupid skin bag! What on earth did you imagine was likely to have happened to me?"

She gulped, searching in vain for a handkerchief.

"I thought you—you might have been —run over, or—or hit on the head, or—"

"Hit on the head!" He looked at her, pityingly. "And just why should you suppose that anyone would *want* to hit me on the head? For crying out loud!" He thrust his own none too clean rag of a handkerchief at her. "Dry your eyes and don't be such a ninny. I thought I'd cured you of this habit? I thought you'd learnt at long last that I'm perfectly capable of looking after myself? How can I be expected to relax and get any enjoyment out of life if I know that you're sitting here weeping like a waterspout and chewing your fingernails to shreds? Great daft loon! Ought to know better, at your age . . . Get those eyes mopped up and maybe I'll take you down the road and stand you a Wimpy—no, damn it, I'm feeling generous: I'll stand you a *double* Wimpy! But only on one condition: only if you give me your solemn, sacred word, Guide's honour, cross your heart and hope to die . . . no more crying over me. How about it? That a bargain?"

She sniffed, but managed a watery smile.

"All right," she said. "It's a bargain."

3

THE talk was all of the new ballet. If opinions before had been sharply divided as to its merits or demerits, opinions now, within the ranks of the Company, were equally divided as to who should dance what and with whom. The part of Adam was the mostly hotly disputed, though most people were in agreement that Nicky and Alex could be the only really serious contenders. Those who supported Nicky did so loudly and vociferously, declaring that the part might almost have been written for him. Those in favour of Alex tended to base their claims more on a general appeal to fair play and a sense of justice. Nicky, they pointed out, could always have his crack at the part later on, when Alex had had a chance to show what could be done with it. It was only right, after all these years, that Alex should be given his opportunity.

Few even amongst Nicky's camp would have denied that Alex deserved an opportunity: *they* simply questioned whether this particular opportunity was the one to give him. Had it been a revival of something classical—a new *Swan Lake*, say, or an updated *Giselle*—then without any doubt at all Alex would have been the man for the job. Look as hard as you like, you couldn't hope to find a more noble Siegfried, a more sympathetic Albrecht. But *Adam*—no, no! A thousand times no! Adam wasn't his sort of part at all. Far too virtuoso, far too extrovert. Alex might be the best and most selfless of partners that anyone could ever wish for, but he didn't have the sheer diamond-hard brilliance to bring off a rôle like Adam.

Perhaps, in their hearts of hearts, even his supporters had just the faintest of misgivings on the point. For all their indignant refutations, one had the feeling it was more from sentiment than from conviction that they argued. Alex was a general favourite throughout the Company—but *could* he bring off a rôle like Adam?

As for the female lead (never specifically named as Eve, but only as "Temptation") it was accepted more or less without question that casting for that would depend almost entirely on whether Madame had sufficient faith in Alex or whether she opted to play safe with Nicky. If Nicky were to be the lucky one, then Gill would no doubt partner him as usual; if Alex, then the choice most likely would fall upon Danielle. Gill found herself torn. The part of Temptation was not one that any ambitious dancer would pass up without a pang, and certainly she would want to dance it opposite no one but Nicky. She couldn't help feeling, on the other hand, that Alex would be most shabbily treated if for a second time he was to be denied his opportunity. But then again, if that meant relinquishing *her* opportunity in favour of Danielle—Danielle of all people in the Company—there were moments when she almost thought she wouldn't care who danced the part so long as it was not that tarted up piece of French frivolity.

She was being unfair, of course. She knew that. She told herself so at least fifty times a day, but somehow it didn't seem to make much difference. She had disliked Danielle almost from the first moment she had set eyes on her. She was not accustomed to dislike people on sight, especially people she had to work with —especially with no apparent cause—but Danielle had roused in her a really quite primitive and wholly unreasoning aversion. She had tried, at first, to put it down to simple jealousy, because jealousy, however despicable, however much it might tear one to pieces, was at least an emotion that one could understand. Not that she cared two straws for the fact of Danielle's being beautiful—other girls in the Company were beautiful. One didn't grudge them that. Still it had come as something of a rude shock to discover that for the first time since she herself had been promoted to soloist, almost three years ago, another had been chosen in her stead to partner Nicky for two of the forthcoming productions. Danielle (*Danielle!* Of all people!) was down to dance opposite him in both *Tricorne*, as the Miller's Wife, and in *Sleeping Beauty*, as the female Bluebird. Certainly it was galling, but honesty, for all that, compelled her to admit that in neither rôle would she be as ideally cast as the French girl—and was she herself not down to dance the Lilac Fairy? And had Madame not faithfully promised that some time in the not too distant future she should be given her chance as Aurora? She could scarcely have any complaints on *that* score. Common sense in any case had always warned her that she could not expect to dance everything with Nicky. In certain spheres, both temperamentally and in points of style, they diverged too widely to be compatible. However much she might like to dream, she knew deep inside herself that when the day came that she was to have that promised chance it would not be with Nicky at her side. Madame would never entrust any young dancer embarking on her first really full-length classical rôle (if you didn't count *Coppélia*) to someone as volatile as Nicky. Far more likely to find herself handed over to the gentle expertise of Alex—which would, she supposed, be something of a comfort. At least with Alex one could relax and feel oneself in perfect safety. She turned her head to look at him across the rehearsal room— and quickly turned it back again. Danielle had perched herself on his lap and was sitting there as bold as brass with her arms twined lovingly about his neck, her chin resting on top of his head. How she did loathe and detest that woman!

She should have been used to it by now. They were already a good ten days into the rehearsal period, and it had taken her no more than the first fifteen minutes of the first morning back to find out the unpalatable truth. Heaven knows, there had been enough people eager to apprise her of it: *Danielle and Alex . . . Alex and Danielle . . .* No use trying to dismiss it as mere dressing-room gossip, the evidence was there for all to see. Whatever Alex's relationship with Danielle might or might not have been over the past three months, it was certainly now something rather more than that of professional colleague. She wouldn't have needed much help in working out that it had been Danielle whom he had put off, for her sake, that first night, but Danielle told her anyway, sunnily informing her of the fact without, apparently, bearing the least grudge in the world.

"So now, *enfin*, I get to meet you . . . ze one 'e take out to dinner instead of me! I 'ave ask 'im, why not all sree of us to go? What you sink 'e say in reply? 'E say two a company, sree a crowd . . . I say sure sree a crowd. Why not we make four? But no! Zis it seem will not do. You are *sa très chère petite* and 'e must 'ave you all to 'imself. I tell to 'im, one more time you do zis and I give you ze big bum rush—bum rush? Zis is right, no? What I mean, I give 'im ze kick up ze pant. It is not very gallant, I sink, to say one make ze crowd."

Maybe not, but it was Gill who bore all the grudges. She resented Danielle as she had never resented any of Alex's previous women. It was, she thought, the sheer brazen cheek of it—the sheer brazen *nerve*. This self-important newcomer, with her flashing teeth and her luminous eyes and her stupid, overdone accent, flaunting in out of nowhere and instantly laying claim, talking of him as if he were her own private property—he was not her private property, he was Gill's property, he was Nicky's property. *They* were the only ones entitled to lay any claims on Alex. Besides, Danielle was not his type. She was far too high-powered, far too much the playgirl. Alex needed someone comfortable and homely, like poor devoted Kath, eating her heart out all to no avail, not this great flouncing sex symbol. Why waste his time on Danielle? What good did he think she was going to do him? Might just as well take up with a painted butterfly.

Out of the corner of her eye, she noticed signs of movement and upheaval.

She knew, without even turning her head, what it was: it was the great sex symbol disengaging its arms from about Alex's neck so that he might prepare himself for his entrance. She kept her eyes fixed firmly to the front, watching as Nicky and some of the rest of the boys were put through their paces. She preferred not to have to look at Danielle and Alex. It made her feel quite sick every time she saw them. It was all so unlike Alex. He had never been one for kissing and cuddling and making an exhibition of himself— not, at any rate, in front of colleagues. Certainly not in a rehearsal studio, of all unsuitable places. Danielle was just making a fool of him. Couldn't keep her hands to herself, that was her trouble. Always had to be touching at him, for ever pecking and poking and draping herself over him. What did she want him for anyway? Why couldn't she go and find someone more in her own league? A prize fighter or a racing driver or an inter-national card sharper, or something.

You'd have thought there were enough men available. Why go and pick on Alex?

From the stiffening of Kath's shoulder against hers, she knew that Kath, too, had sensed the disengaging. Of course, it was even worse for Kath. She had been helplessly in love with Alex for years. Gill had often thought of telling him so, except that Kath had made her swear on her honour that she never, ever would.

"If he doesn't notice me he doesn't notice me and that's all there is to it. I'd die of shame if you breathed so much as a word."

It was sad how even someone so essentially caring as Alex could be hurtful without realizing. One day, she thought, she would draw it to his attention in spite of her promise to Kath. Alex wasn't the sort to stand by in silence and do nothing whilst a fellow human being suffered. He would surely feel *some*thing in return for such devotion? Only let that Danielle grow tired of her games and remove herself from the scene—

"Pardon me," said Kath. She suddenly

shot to her feet with such vigour that Gill, deprived of her supportive shoulder, almost fell over. "I feel a rather urgent call to go to the farthest end of the studio."

"What? What urgent call? What are you—"

Too late: Kath was off and she was trapped. Danielle was already there, already happily settling herself down in the vacated space. Rather like Nicky, Danielle was not a person who ever stopped to ask herself whether her presence might not be welcome; she took it for granted that it must be.

"*Buon giorno!*" she said, gaily. "*Comment ça va?*"

Yes, and that was another thing: why the constant need to babble in half a dozen different languages? Showing off, no doubt. Well, it wouldn't get her far if she tried it on with Alex. Boys dragged out of homes were lucky if they learnt to speak their own language correctly, let alone anyone else's. But then, of course, when she was with Alex she probably didn't bother saying anything at all. When she was with him she would have better things to do.

Gill said "Good morning" as ungraciously as she could, which wasn't as ungracious as it might have been on account of the fact that Danielle, however much one might tell oneself that one despised and abominated her, was not the easiest of persons to be ungracious to.

"You know," she now said to Gill, with the air of one about to impart a great confidence, "what I should like most to be doing at zis moment?"

"No," said Gill. She was more interested in watching Nicky perform a series of rather spectacular turns than being admitted to the innermost sanctum of Danielle's secret yearnings. "What?" she said, with a grudging attempt at politeness.

Danielle sent both arms snaking up above her head and stretched, with sinuous voluptuousness, like a cat. Even wearing hideous pink practice sweater and thick woolly leg warmers she somehow managed to look coquettish.

"I should like," she said. "to be in bed wiz Aleex." (In bed wiz Aleex! It was enough to make anyone squirm.) "I should like 'im to be making love wiz me. We shall go on all ze day, all ze night—"

Gill turned slowly to look at her out of grave eyes.

"All the day *and* all the night?"

"*Mais oui! Pourquoi pas?* 'E is verree good at it. Does zat surprise you per'aps just a leetle?"

It did, perhaps—just a little. Not that she would have admitted it. Not to Danielle.

"I should have thought," she said, crushingly, "that he would have dropped dead with exhaustion long before night came."

"Oh, don' worry—I will give 'im ze leetle rest in between." Danielle smiled, complacently, and sunk her chin into the neck of her sweater. "When I first join ze Company, I take a look about myself and I say, where is ze man, Danielle, 'oo is

79

ze one for you . . . Zere are not so many men, you know. Not—" she waved a hand—"in zis meadow. You say meadow?"

"Field, actually," said Gill.

"*Ah, bon!* Zis field, *alors*. Not so many, *hein?* Zey are 'alf of zem—*comment dites vous? Un peu—*"

"Quite," said Gill.

István was sitting within earshot and she saw no reason to offend him. He couldn't help being as he was.

"*Et alors*, I take one look at Aleex and I sink, zat is ze one for you, Danielle . . . I nevair make mistake, you know."

"I'm sure you don't," said Gill.

Looking them over as if they were a herd of prize bulls—just as well Nicky hadn't been there. She turned back again to watch him as he came to the end of his variation. Danielle, following the direction of her gaze, said: "*Il est beau, n'est-ce pas? Vraiment très beau.* You tell me—" she leaned forward, her head close to Gill's— "'ow is 'e like, your leetle Nicky? I sink 'e mus' be much fun, no?"

Gill felt her cheeks begin to glow bright scarlet—whether with rage or confusion she could not be sure. Danielle was impossible. Really quite impossible. " *'Ow is 'e like*"—what sort of a question was that? Did the woman honestly imagine that she was going to discuss Nicky's most intimate qualities with a complete stranger?

"Oh, mon Dieu!" Danielle clapped a hand to her mouth. Her eyes widened, dramatically. "I am treading wiz my feet in it, *non? Excusez-moi, chérie*—I 'ad not realized. I sink because you live wiz 'im —ah!" She beat at her forehead with clenched fist. "*Stupide Danielle!* Aleex 'as tell to me already . . . 'e is your cousin, *n'est-ce pas? Bien sûr*, zat is no reason for itself, *mais*—"

Down at the far end of the studio, Kath was sitting grinning like a gnome with her knees hugged into her chest. Gill scrambled rather pointedly to her feet.

"Excuse me," she said. "I must go and speak to Kath . . . I've just remembered something I have to tell her."

That evening, after rehearsal, as they walked home together to Guilford Street, she asked Nicky what he thought of Danielle. He grinned and said: "Bit of a goer, by all accounts . . . poor old Alexis! I bet he's still wondering what's hit him. He'll never last the season out, the way she's putting him through it."

"Alex knows how to look after himself," said Gill.

"He certainly ought to . . . had enough experience! Mind you, I don't suppose he's ever had a bird like this take a shine to him before."

"Why not?" said Gill. "He's very good at it—Danielle told me."

"Did she, indeed?" Nicky chuckled happily to himself. "She should know, if anyone does!"

Gill was silent a moment.

"Do you find her—" she hesitated— "seductive?" she said.

"Me? You must be joking!"

"Everyone else seems to."

"Yeah, well—she's not my sort, is she?"

"Isn't she?" She looked at him, hopefully. "What is your sort?"

He might have laughed and ruffled her hair and said: "Why, you are, of course!" It would have been a comfort, even if only in jest. Instead, as they turned in at the street door, he said: "Oh, something big and blonde and buxom . . . something with a bit of flesh on it. That's the trouble with all you little sylphlike creatures . . . might be a feast for sore eyes flitting about a stage in pink satin and bits of gauze, but you haven't any substance. All so damned skinny. Like trying to get to grips with a bag full of old chicken bones. Now, you take our Trudi . . . there's a fine figure of a woman for you. *That's* what I should call a nice handful. Something you can get hold of with that one."

"I see," said Gill. She forced herself to give a little smile. She couldn't be jealous of Trudi—not *Trudi*. Why, she was old enough to be his mother. "You must be the only man in the Company," she said, "who hasn't got his tongue hanging out."

"Oh, I don't know." Cheerfully, he

flung open the door of the flat. "I haven't noticed István exactly panting at her heels."

"I said the only *man*," said Gill.

"Ah-uh!" He wagged a finger at her. "Don't be catty. Anyway, the lady for the time being belongs to Alexis. You wouldn't have me poach on his preserves, would you?"

She wouldn't have him poach on anyone's preserves. She only wished—oh! how she did wish—that he would take notice occasionally of what was right here on his own doorstep. She picked up the milk and carried it out with her to the kitchen. Nicky had gone straight through to the bathroom. She could already hear the bath taps running. Her heart sank. When the first thing he did on arriving home was turn the bath on—

"No towels!" He strode back again into the living-room. "All the towels have gone. What have you done with them?"

"I haven't done anything with them. It's laundry day. Manuela's been up."

"So where have they gone, then?"

"To the laundry, I should hope."

"No, you great pillock! The clean ones."

"The clean ones," she said, "will be in the cupboard. Where they always are."

"Oh."

He turned back. She followed him, standing at the open door.

"Are you—going out again?"

He had been out every night for the past week—making the most, no doubt, of free evenings while they still had them. There must have been an unintentional note of wistfulness in her voice. Nicky paused, in the act of taking a bath towel from the cupboard. She wondered, idly, without really caring, why he had to choose one from right at the very bottom of the pile when it would be so much easier to take the one off the top.

"I had thought of it," he said. "Why?"

"Oh, no reason. I just wondered. I just like to know, so I can—can decide about food."

He frowned.

"What are *you* going to do with yourself?"

"I hadn't made up my mind. Have an early night, I expect."

"Why don't you pop over and see Alex?"

"What for? I've already seen him. In any case, he's probably tucked up in bed with Danielle by now. He wouldn't thank *me* for disturbing him."

She went back to the kitchen. There weren't even any breakfast dishes to wash up: Manuela, out of the goodness of her heart and her maternal penchant for Nicky, had already done them. She had done the ironing, as well, and made both the beds. Really there wasn't anything left at all. Nicky had appeared again at the kitchen door. He was still holding the bath towel in his hands.

"You could always go and spend the evening with Kath," he said.

She turned on him, in sudden fury.

"Why should I go and spend the evening with Kath? You think I'm incapable, or something? Why shouldn't

I just spend the evening here at home, if that's what I want to do? I don't try running your life for you: don't you try running mine!"

Before he left, he knocked at the door of her room—most unusual formality—and putting his head round said: "Gilly, I'm off . . . Don't wait up for me, I don't know what time I'll be back. It may not be till late. And Gilly—if it isn't till late, you won't go getting in one of your states, will you? There's a good girl."

When Nicky had gone, she telephoned Kath. She wasn't having him feel sorry for her, she wasn't having him feel himself obliged to suggest things she might do, but in fact an evening spent with Kath was not such a bad idea. They could at least have a good moan together about Danielle, if nothing else.

Kath lived in Highbury. It was only ten minutes away by tube on the Victoria Line. She lived with her parents because it was convenient and because in any case she was that sort of a girl—quiet, gentle, home-loving. Just exactly the sort of girl who would do for Alex, if only he could be persuaded to see it.

When Gill arrived, the family were all sitting in a semi-circle watching television in the half-light. Kath took her upstairs to her own room, with its pretty chintzy curtains and pink candlewick bedspread. On the bedside table was a studio portrait of Alex looking romantic in his Sylphide costume with his hair grown long. It was a publicity photograph from a couple of seasons ago which somehow or other she had managed to filch. It was, it had to be admitted, a very handsome photograph— but of what comfort could a mere photo-graph be, when the original seemed scarcely even aware of your existence? Gill sat herself down on the hearth rug before the electric fire with its imitation coal. Kath didn't sit anywhere at all but walked about the room in a nervous fashion picking up china ornaments and putting them down again. It wasn't like Kath to be nervous. She was usually very placid, very composed.

"I'm glad you came," she said. "It gives me an opportunity to—"

She paused.

"To what?" said Gill.

Kath drew a deep breath.

"I've got something to tell you . . . I nearly wrote it you, then I thought that would be cowardly. I've been trying to pluck up courage ever since you got back."

Gill looked up, solemn-eyed.

"Is it something I'm not going to like?"

"It's something you're probably not even going to believe . . . The fact is, I'm—" She blushed slightly, and attempted a smile. "I'm going to marry my stockbroker."

"What!" Gill rocketed back on her heels. Kath marry her stockbroker? It wasn't possible! Kath's stockbroker had been a joke between them for almost as long as she could remember. He was her Dobbin, her standby, her going-out-for-a-drink-with when all else had failed. She couldn't marry *him*. Alex in his Sylphide costume looking down at her from the bedside table and she in all seriousness proposing to marry a stockbroker?

"I know," said Kath. "I can read it in your eyes. You don't have to tell me. But let's face it, the ballet isn't going to miss me and I can't go on like this for the rest of my life. There comes a time when you have to wake up and stop daydreaming —and I woke up about two months ago somewhere on the Great North Road. Somewhere between Huddersfield and Hartlepool . . . I just knew then that I couldn't take any more of it."

Gill pursed her lips.

"It's that Danielle, isn't it?" she said. "Getting her claws into him."

"Oh, if you could have *seen* her!" Kath banged down a little glass animal with a vehemence she very rarely displayed. "Practically raping him in *front* of everyone."

"And him, of course, just lapping it up?"

"Well, what man wouldn't?" Kath, even now, was quick to leap to his defence. "*He* couldn't help it. It's not his fault if she makes a dead set at him."

"He didn't have to respond."

"And why shouldn't he?"

"Oh, Kath!" Gill looked at her, reproachfully. "You don't have to go marrying your stockbroker just because of this. You know it won't last—not with a girl like Danielle."

"Don't you see? I don't care whether it lasts or not—I simply don't care any more. I've lived in cloud cuckoo land long enough. Why go on deceiving myself? If ever he *were* going to look twice at me he'd have done it by this time—it just makes me so absolutely furious to think that *she* can come marching along and get exactly what she wants out of him simply by fluttering her false eyelashes while I've been sitting about like a great lemon all these years and never once—never *once* —oh, what's the use?" She flung herself on to the bed. "What does it matter, anyway? One man's probably just the same as another."

Gill sat silent on the hearthrug, staring

into the bars of the electric fire with its rhythmic flickering behind the painted coal. *She* didn't think one man was just the same as another—but then she had been luckier than Kath. Just a little. *Never once*, Kath had said. *Never once* . . . But Nicky, once—even if it *were* only the once—it still made her luckier than Kath. It did give her something to hold on to as hope for the future. At least *once* Nicky had noticed that she was there. It was the night on which he had first taken her to Vic and Trudi's—the night he had flirted with Trudi, and Vic had told her to "watch that lad, if I were you, when he gets you back home." It had been four o'clock in the morning when they arrived back in Guilford Street and Nicky had made love to her. It was the very first time that anyone ever had, but Nicky hadn't realized until afterwards, when she herself had shyly confessed it to him. He had seemed a bit taken aback. He had said "Christ" and run a hand through his hair; and then, almost accusingly: "Why didn't you *tell*

me?" Somehow, she had always assumed
that he must have known. It was so inconceivable to her that she should ever do
such a thing with anyone else that she had
taken it for granted it must be equally
inconceivable to him. She had often
wondered, since, what difference it would
have made if she had told him. Maybe
then he would never have done it at all,
and she, like Kath, would be saying
"never once".

"While we're on the subject—" Kath
rolled over on to her side, chin propped
on hand—"how about you? How long do
you intend to go on waiting?"

The ready blush sprang to Gill's
cheeks. Kath was something of a privi-
leged person, the only one with whom she
ever had discussed or ever would discuss
her feelings for Nicky; but there were
limits beyond which even Kath should
know better than to transgress. Kath
shook her head; not unkindly.

"It's no use getting all red and angry
with me. *I*'ve had to face facts—it's about
time you did. Honestly, Gilly . . . you

can't hang around indefinitely. You can't go *on* being little Gill who's always available. People get used to things, you know. They take things for granted. The longer you leave it, the more difficult it's going to be—and the less likely you are to get what you're after. If you really want that boy to sit up and take notice you're going to have to do something about it."

There was a pause; then Gill said: "Such as what?"

"Such as almost anything—it can hardly fail to be better than nothing. You might do worse than spend a few days observing our *femme fatale*. Learn a bit of her technique—put it into practice. Only on Nicky, of course. I'm not suggesting you have to go around seducing half the Company."

Gill looked down at the rug on which she was sitting. It was orange and peacock blue. She had never noticed before how violently it clashed with the bedspread.

"Well?" said Kath.

Gill kept her gaze upon the rug.

"It isn't any use," she said.

"What isn't?"

"What you suggested."

"Why not? What's wrong with it?"

"Nothing, except that—that I couldn't do it, that's all."

"What do you mean, you couldn't do it? Couldn't seduce *Nicky?*" There was an amused chuckle from the direction of the bed. "I shouldn't have thought *he*'d have given anyone much bother!"

No; she was quite sure that he wouldn't. The only problem was that she wasn't anyone. She said as much to Kath, who instantly seized upon it.

"No, you're not anyone, you're *you*. That's the whole point. That's exactly what you've got to make him see. You're you in your own right, not just some convenient doormat that's been lying around for as long as he can remember."

"Yes, and me in my own right wouldn't even know where to begin! It's no *use* telling me to do a Danielle on him. I couldn't, I'm not the type. I haven't any talent that way. How could I have? Look at me!"

Kath looked.

"So what's the matter with you?"

"What's the *matter* with me?" She sprang to her feet, facing the dressing-table. "I'm just a bag of old chicken bones, that's what's the matter with me! You'd hardly call me a *nice handful*, would you?"

"You know, now you come to mention it," said Kath, "I never *did* see you in the role of Temptation."

"Oh, that! That's different. That's dancing. I can do anything if I can *dance* it."

"Yes, well, dancing's not very likely to help you in this situation," said Kath, brutally blunt. "But I can tell you one thing . . . you'd better try making *some* kind of an effort, and you'd better try making it pretty damn quickly if you don't fancy the idea of old Gorgeous Gussie turning her great big frog's eyes in a direction rather nearer home."

"She's not his sort," said Gill.

"She wasn't Alex's," retorted Kath, "and look what's happened to him . . .

just don't you ever dare turn round to me and say you haven't been warned, that's all."

The following day they had a run-through of the Prologue and Act I of *Sleeping Beauty*. Alex, not being required until later in the ballet, had not been called—the general consensus was that he didn't know his own good fortune. It was a grim rehearsal. Madame was in one of her more finicking moods, when nothing and no one could please her and not even Nicky could charm her out of it. She kept them there, sweating and straining, until almost seven o'clock, and even then quellingly informed them that they danced with about as much vitality as a herd of hippopotamus.

"Lurid," said Derek. "Just lurid."

The entire day had been rather lurid. Not once, but several times, had Gill been forced to witness the displeasing spectacle of Danielle, in default of Alex to snuggle up to, draping herself over Nicky, twining herself round *his* neck, seating herself on *his* lap. The worst of it was, that Nicky played up to it—and small comfort to reflect that Nicky always did play up, that unlike Alex he was perfectly ready to disport himself in public, to have a bit of a kiss and a cuddle with anyone who cared to offer it him. Danielle was not anyone, any more than Gill herself. Gill was little Gill who was always available and consequently never wanted: Danielle was a disruptive force who had already bent Alex to her will and now looked set to bend Nicky likewise. At least Kath had the tact not to say anything.

The only bright spot in an otherwise dismal day was that Nicky, as if by way of a peace offering, decided for once to pass an evening at home. Unfortunately, having done so, he quite plainly had not the least idea how to occupy himself but spent the entire first hour after dinner fretfully prowling to and fro about the flat like a caged panther. Gill, nervous of suggesting anything lest it might provoke him into a sudden change of heart, sat on the sofa mending holes in tights. She knew it was scarcely a very alluring pastime—she knew that Kath would not have approved. *You'd better try making SOME kind of an effort . . .* but what? What was she supposed to do? Throw down her mending and tear off all her clothes? Go and twine herself about his neck and slobber over him like a Danielle? He would think she had run mad. The sad truth was that he simply didn't look at her in that light. If he had made love to her once it had been because he was feeling irresponsible, because he had had a good evening and a bit to drink, because she was the only woman available—for whatever reason, it had not been because she was Gill in her own right. Next morning he had behaved as if nothing had happened.

It was how he had been behaving ever since. Surely if she had had any natural talent—

"For crying out loud!" Nicky suddenly twitched impatiently at the pair of tights she was mending. "Put that rubbish away and do something to entertain me."

She was only too willing. She pushed the tights at once down the back of the sofa.

"What would you like to do?"

"I don't know! I'm asking you."

"We could always try listening to the music for *Adam*. I borrowed the record off Alex yesterday. It's something or other by Webern, he says it takes a bit of getting used to. I thought we ought at least to hear it through—just in case."

It was a suggestion which appealed. They heard the record through a good half dozen times, discussing possibilities, exchanging ideas, familiarizing themselves with the music, until at last Nicky said "What the hell! We could just be tantalizing ourselves . . . turn the thing over. Let's hear what's on the other side."

The other side was Schoenberg, *Verklaerte Nacht*. It was lush and romantic after the sparseness of the Webern. It seemed for a while to lull even Nicky into restfulness.

She felt him slowly beginning to relax, to unwind, to lose some of that live-wire tenseness that was so much a part of him. *Verklaerte Nacht!* Transfigured night . . . the night could be transfigured even yet. Nicky himself could transfigure it quite easily, if only he would. She rested her head against his shoulder. He let it stay there, idly running his fingers through her hair. Any form of caress, however casual, coming from Nicky, was precious to her. It happened so rarely—he so rarely remained still for long enough. She lay back against him, fearful even of breathing too deeply lest the spell might be broken. What, she wondered, would Danielle do in such a situation? *She* surely wouldn't just lie there, passive? Surely Danielle, in some way, would respond? Perhaps when the record had finished—

The record was given no chance to finish. Before they were even half way through, Nicky was back on his feet again.

"This thing's enough to send anyone into a coma! It's like flaming Delius—

nothing ever happens. Tell you what—"
With two quick strides he was across the
room, switching off the record player,
taking the record off the turntable. "I just
remembered, there's a party over at
Zoë's. Go and grab your coat and let's
shove off there. We can pick up a bottle
on the way. . . come on! Chop chop!"
Clapping his hands, he chivvied her to her
feet and across the room. "Get your
skates on! Can't sit here doing nothing all
night."

4

"OK, fine. That's coming along. You're getting the hang of it. Try softening the line slightly—curve the arms . . . let them droop . . . now the head—like so—and the eyes—right! That's it! That's much better. Let's take it again from the beginning—and just bear in mind that you're meant to be seducing him, not turning the poor chap to stone. The name of the game is Temptation . . . all right? Right—"

It was almost a fortnight, now, since the casting for *Adam* had been announced. Madame had played safe, as most people had predicted she would: Nicky was to dance Adam, Gill was to partner him. More than one person, during the past few days, had come up to Alex in private with indignant expostulations on his behalf, saying that it was damned unfair and wasn't there any justice left in the world, but much though he might have welcomed the chance to show what he could do with the part he had known from the outset that there was small enough likelihood of his being given it. No false sentiment about Madame, not when her Company's reputation was at stake. It had come as no great surprise when she had broken the news to him— and after searching his conscience pretty thoroughly he felt he could put his hand to his heart and say in all honesty that he did not resent her final choice. It was probably the same one that he would have made had he been in her position. The piece in itself was sufficient of a gamble; why run more risk than she had to?

Rehearsals had started a week ago. Nicky had mastered immediately not only the fairly complex choreography but the whole style and mood of the ballet—as his supporters had so rightly claimed, the part might almost have been written for him. Gill, for some reason, was having more difficulty. It was not so much the steps themselves that were causing her any problems as the interpretation. She understood well enough what was wanted, he was quite sure of that; she simply seemed unable for once to translate it into terms of movement. It was puzzling, because it was not like Gill. She who in general was so fluid, so pliant, so receptive to the smallest nudge in the right direction, had of a sudden closed up, had become stiff, almost self-conscious. There were those in the Company, he was aware, who had all along considered Danielle to be the more obvious choice. He was the one who had pressed for Gill, maintaining that her more virginal charms, her purity of line, her slightly withdrawn quality, would both counter-balance and complement the overt sensuality of the choreography. Danielle, he had insisted, would be too much of a good thing. It would be like adding treacle to whipped cream. Gill had just that edge of sharpness which would bring out the full flavour. Madame in the end had allowed herself to be persuaded—at least in some spheres, it seemed, she was prepared to trust him. He for his part had never had any doubts. He had believed from the start that Gill was the right choice, he believed it even now, even in despite of this unexpected, and as far as he was concerned totally inexplicable, mental block that had assailed her. It was troublesome, certainly; but one way or another he intended to crack it.

Thinking to help, he had offered to give up the whole of his Sunday morning and afternoon to running her through as much of the part as he had so far taught her. She had accepted the offer, but hesitantly, almost as it seemed to him reluctantly. There had been none of her usual bright eagerness. She had said "Yes, all right—I suppose we ought. When do you want me to turn up? About eleven?"

That in itself would have been sufficient to convince him, if by now he had needed any convincing, that all was not well. When in addition, however, she had categorically vetoed the suggestion that Nicky should come along with her, he had known there must be something, somewhere, very wrong indeed. That the two of them had not fallen out seemed obvious from their behaviour, which continued no different from usual—and anyway, it was hard to imagine anyone ever falling out with Nicky. Goaded beyond endurance, he had tried it himself on more than one occasion: he had never yet been able to manage it. A soft answer turneth away wrath, but Nicky had only to smile—and if even *he* succumbed, what hope was there for Gill? No, they had not fallen out, but still there was something that needed investigation; something personal that was coming between her and the ballet.

"Look, sweetheart—" He stopped her again. He had to: there was nothing there. He tried making light of it, hoping still that with patience and perseverance he might be able to work her through it, unlock the key to whatever it was that was holding her back. "This is a sexy lady you're supposed to be portraying—not first cousin to Medusa! Come on, now, let yourself go. Try thinking lascivious thoughts—and don't tell me you've never had any, because I refuse to believe it! All this wide-eyed innocence might take other people in, but it doesn't deceive me . . . I've lived with you too long. Why, I've heard you say things would make an Irish navvy break into a sweat! Let's go through it one more time—and this time I want to be made to feel uncomfortable; OK?" He winked at her. "You can always try pretending I'm Nicky, if it makes it any easier."

All too obviously, it did not. After only a few seconds she broke off.

"This is hopeless! We're just wasting our time—why do we bother to go on? Anyone can see that I'm not right for the part."

"Oh?" He raised an eyebrow. "That says a lot for my judgement."

"Oh, Alex, don't be angry! I don't *want* to let you down, it's just that it's—well, it's not *me*."

"In what way is it not you?"

"Every way! I'm *not* a sexy lady, I'm

a totally *un*sexy lady . . . I haven't got any magnetism—I haven't got any wiles."

"You think not?"

"Well, *look* at me!"

He looked at her, standing there before him, a little insubstantial wisp of a thing in chaste black leotard and tights, hair pulled back, dark eyes burning in the pale face. She had wiles enough for him—she always had had. He could remember even now how as a tiny child she had clambered on to his knee and clasped both arms round his neck and pressed her cheek against his as an animal sign of affection. It had been the first real affection that he had ever known. Perhaps that was the very reason she had such power over him.

"I'm looking at you," he said. He smiled. "There might not be a great deal of you, but—"

"There isn't *any*thing of me! Just a bag of old chicken bones! How could I be expected to seduce anyone? Probably couldn't even seduce a sex-starved gorilla on a desert island."

"That," he said, "is a very silly statement."

"All right, then!" She turned on him, half it seemed as a challenge, half almost as a plea. "If you think I'm so right for the part why don't you show me? Why don't you prove it to me? Show me how it's done—give me a practical demonstration! You're supposed to be the one who's teaching me, aren't you? Well, go on, then . . . teach me!"

It took a moment or so for it to sink in: she was actually demanding of him that he make love to her. She actually wanted him to do it for real. He had thought he had been around too long, had seen too much, to be shocked any more; but that, coming from Gill, quite took him aback. Anyone else and he would not have batted an eyelid. Danielle or Andrea, Tanya or Zoë, even that funny old mother hen of a Kath with her big moon face and her thighs like giant oaks; but *Gill*—Why turn to him and not to Nicky? Nicky was the one she loved, Nicky was the one she lived with. Why not go to him? Unless, of course—

He stood frowning, gazing down at her. Unless, of course, the wretched boy had gone and made a mess of things? He wouldn't put it past him, slapdash as he was. But if that were the case, then he deserved to be kicked all the way from here to kingdom come. He didn't doubt but that Gill would need a lot of love and tenderness. She was no Danielle to be picked up and put down again as the fancy took one. But by the same token, Nicky was no raw youth. He ought by now to know what he was about. If after all this time, with all his physical advantages, blessed as he was with an abundance of charm and good looks, he had not yet learnt how to handle a delicate flower like Gill, then there wasn't very much hope for him. There were some problems it wasn't any use bringing to dear old Alex, because dear old Alex couldn't solve them. At another time, in other circumstances—if she were to come to him because she wanted *him*; but he was damned if he was going to do Nicky's love-making for him by proxy.

"You see?" said Gill. "I told you so."

"What do you mean, you told me so?"

"I told you I wasn't right for the part . . . if I were, you wouldn't be looking so embarrassed."

"For heaven's sake!" He pushed a lock of hair out of his eyes. "I'm not embarrassed. I'm just—slightly thrown off balance."

"I don't see why you should be. From all I hear you're something of a cross between Casanova and Rudolph Valentino."

"Yes," he said, modestly. He grinned, glad of the chance for a bit of light relief. "That sounds like me, all right. Now, what is all this nonsense in aid of? Someone been pumping Stanislavski into you, or what? I suppose if you were dancing Giselle you wouldn't actually insist on being driven mad before you could tackle the part, would you?"

"No, but this is different. I *told* you.

I just don't have any natural talent this way."

"Whereas, of course, when it comes to going mad—"

"Oh, Alex, don't tease! I'm serious! One can't be good at everything, and I'm obviously not good at *this*. If you really want me to do the part properly, then you'll just have to teach me how."

And how easily he could. How fatally easily. He could take her into his arms right now. He could lead her across to the studio couch, he could—

He turned away.

"Don't be ridiculous," he said.

"What's ridiculous about it? You don't have any objections to teaching *other* people, do you? I bet if Danielle were here you wouldn't have any objections to teaching her—except that Danielle wouldn't need any teaching, would she? She already knows all there is to know."

"Danielle," he said, grimly, "already knows a great deal more than is good for her to know."

"Then she ought to have been given

113

the part instead of me! She could obviously do it far better than I can. She—"

"Gilly!" He spun back again, catching her by the shoulders. "Will you please stop this cretinous babbling? If you'll just have a bit of confidence in yourself you'll do the part a thousand times better than Danielle, experience or no experience."

"But I *need* the experience! I—"

"You do not need the experience! Not, at any rate, from me." Not, at any rate, in *these* circumstances. "You go to Nicky and ask him."

She pursed her lips.

"You mean that you won't?"

"That is exactly what I mean."

"I see." She tilted her chin. "You don't mind doing it with other people. You don't mind doing it with Danielle. You—"

"For crying out loud!" He shook her slightly. "What are you talking about, you stupid girl? You are not Danielle, you are not other people, you're you; and the way I treat you is not the same way I treat everyone else!"

114

"Well, that's a pity, isn't it?" she said. There was a break in her voice as she said it. In spite of himself, he was very sorely tempted to pull her towards him and demonstrate once and for all, let there be no mistake about it, that the way he would treat her was a million miles removed from the cavalier fashion in which he treated the Danielles of this world; but then, in the background, there was always Nicky. He thought: *I could murder that boy . . . I could cheerfully put my hands round his neck and I could strangle him . . .* What in God's name had he done to her to reduce her to such a state as this?

"Now, you listen," he said. "You just listen a minute to what I'm going to tell you . . . firstly, get this into your head: whatever difficulties you're having, they've got nothing to do with your dancing. I don't want any more excuses about not being right for the part. The *part* has got nothing to do with it. Secondly, it takes two people to make a hash of things. Right? So whatever's going wrong, you can take it from me, it's Nicky's fault just as much as it is yours. Don't kid yourself he's perfect, because he isn't. Very far from it. And thirdly—" He hesitated, not sure just how far it was up to him to encroach on other people's territory. Without knowing the full circumstances, he could just as easily put his foot in it as not. And then again, with Nicky—the fact was, one could never be a hundred per cent certain. There was too much ambivalence, too many unanswered questions. Short of asking him outright—but he never had been one to tolerate interference. He certainly wouldn't thank Alex for coming the heavy father. *What exactly are your intentions, young man?* The chances were, being Nicky, he probably didn't even have any intentions. He just took life as it came, living it from day to day. If anyone were going to put intentions into his head, it would have to be Gill herself. No one else could do it for her. Much as Alex might yearn to see her happy and laughing again, the way she had always used to be, before she went to live with Nicky, there was nothing he could actually do that would bring it about. He could only wait around and make sure that he was on hand to pick up the pieces, if pieces there were, at the close of the day.

Gill was looking up at him, plainly waiting for him to continue.

"And thirdly?"

"Thirdly—" Thirdly, it was none of his damned business anyway. "Tell me," he said. "Young Lothario . . . is he going to be in tonight?"

She hunched her shoulders.

"I don't know."

Didn't *know?* He studied her, more closely.

"Gilly, you haven't gone and quarrelled with each other, have you?"

"Quarrelled?" She sounded indignant. "We don't *quarrel!*"

"Oh—well. All right, then. I just wondered . . . Anyway, if he *is* going to be in, you know what I suggest you do? I suggest you try telling him what you've told me—try telling *him* why you're having difficulties. It's about time that boy stopped being selfish and pulled his finger out and started to think of someone other than number one for a change—yes, and you needn't look at me like that. You know as well as I do that it's true. You just go back there and start making a few demands on him for once. Might shake him out of his complacency—wake him up to the fact that you've got needs as well as him. Do him a world of good. And just remember . . . no more nonsense about not being able to do it. Next rehearsal I want to see results."

Nicky was still indoors when she arrived back from Clapham. She found him crawling round the living-room floor wearing nothing but his socks and a pair of bright red underpants, pressing some trousers with a damp tea towel. He was standing the iron in the hearth and was using one of the blankets from his bed as an ironing cloth. They had a perfectly good ironing board in the kitchen cupboard. She wondered, with a flash of irritation, why he didn't get it out. Couldn't be bothered, no doubt. In a hurry to go somewhere, and simply grabbed at the first materials that came to hand. That was Nicky all over. She was only surprised that he should be troubling to press trousers at all. What was wrong with the old blue jeans and the safety pin? He glanced up, casually, as she came in.

"Back already? I thought you'd be staying the night. So how'd it go?"

"All right," she said.

"Got it together at last, have you?"

"Got what together?"

"Well, actually, I was referring to the *part*, but—"

"Oh, were you?" she said.

"Yes, I was. . . scout's honour, miss . . . cross me 'eart and 'ope to die . . . Why, anyway?" He set the iron back with a cheerful thud in the fireplace. "Did you think I might be referring to something else?"

"I had no idea *what* you might be referring to."

"OK, OK! So for you I speak plain English . . . seriously. You feeling any happier with things now?"

"Since you ask," she said, "the answer has to be no. I'm not." She remembered what Alex had said. *It takes two people to make a hash of things . . . Whatever's going wrong, you can take it from me, it's Nicky's fault just as much as it is yours . . .* She trod her way ostentatiously round the perimeter of the blanket and across to her own room. "In the circumstances," she said, "it's hardly very surprising."

She slammed the door behind her, tore off her coat, sat herself down with a thump before the dressing-table. Her face, white and drawn and faintly tragic, stared out at her from the glass. *What am I to do?* she thought. *What AM I to do?*

The door opened and Nicky appeared.

"What's the problem?" he said. "What's got you so uptight all of a sudden? Nothing I've done, is it?"

"No," she said. "*Nothing* you've done."

"Well, that's a relief!" He closed the door behind him and wandered across to the dressing-table, leaning against it in his red underpants, grinning down at her. "So what is it? Something's got your goat . . . . never tell me it's old Alexis going and forgetting himself and making an ungentlemanly pass at you after all these years?"

It was as much as she could do to keep from throwing something at him. She turned, deliberately, and picked up her hair brush.

"Don't be so stupid."

"Nothing stupid about it. What's stupid? Why shouldn't he make a pass at you? Wonder of it is he's managed to restrain himself as long as he has. It's my belief—" he suddenly leaned forward and peered at his face in the dressing-table mirror—"that he's more than half in love with you. Whether he *knows* it or not—" He ran a hand over his chin. "Hell! Do I need to shave?"

She took the question as rhetorical and made no answer. Why ask *her* if he needed to shave? It entirely depended, she would have thought, on whom he was going to meet and what he was going to do with them when he'd met them.

"What do you reckon?" He rubbed his cheek against hers. "Doesn't feel like sandpaper, does it?"

Actually it did, but maliciously she said: "No. Feels all right to me." At least she would have the satisfaction of knowing that whoever it was he was going to meet would be in for a rough time of it. With any luck it would be someone with an extremely sensitive skin. Not that it was all that much of a satisfaction—it even made her feel just the tiniest bit mean. She was on the point of repenting and saying that well, perhaps after all he ought, when abruptly he abandoned the problem of his chin and reached out a hand for her one remaining quarter ounce bottle of very expensive scent that Alex had given her the previous Christmas.

"Whether he *knows* it or not—" he took a cautious sniff—"is, of course, a different matter. The chances are he probably doesn't. Chances are that even if he does he'd sooner not admit it. But I bet you a pound to a pinch of pigstuff—" calmly, he tipped up the bottle—"that that's how it is. Bet you any money you like. Shouldn't be at all surprised if—"

"*Will* you stop wasting my Yves St. Laurent?" Outraged, Gill banged down her hairbrush and snatched at the bottle before he could use up every last precious drop. "Go out and buy your own scent—and stop talking nonsense about Alex!"

"It's not nonsense. I'm telling you, he—" He broke off, affronted, and wrinkled his nose. "Jesus wept! That stuff's pretty powerful, isn't it? I smell like a whore at a flaming christening!"

"Serves you right. You're not supposed to *bath* in it. And anyway, it is nonsense."

It had to be nonsense. It couldn't be anything but. If Alex were even only the littlest bit in love with her—which she didn't believe for an instant—he would surely have seized the opportunity when it was offered? Had she not practically *begged* him? And still he hadn't raised so much as a finger—hadn't even been tempted. Nicky didn't know what he was talking about. That was typical of Nicky. Expound on any subject under the sun, all the way from nuclear physics to Zen Buddhism, given half the chance. The fact that he was totally *ignorant*—besides, what about Danielle? What about all the others? Nicky reached forward, clawed up a handful of tissues, unceremoniously spat on them and began rubbing at his chest.

"Why else do you suppose he puts it around so much?"

"Puts what around?" She was startled. Surely to goodness Alex hadn't been going about *telling* people he was in love with her? That she most certainly would not believe. He wouldn't do that even if he were. "What about Danielle?" she said.

"That's what I mean . . . why else do you imagine he hops about like a flea on hot bricks? Let's face it . . . old Alexis, he's a bit of a home-loving lad. He's not exactly the sort you'd *expect* to find adventuring through half the beds in London, is he?"

"Well—"

"Course he's not. Going against all that nature intended. So why does he do it? What's the reason?"

She looked at him, doubtfully. Had she herself not already pondered that very same question?

"I'll tell you what the reason is. Because, I reckon—" disdainfully, amidst a rising aroma of Yves St. Laurent, Nicky began picking out the myriad multi-coloured flakes of disintegrated tissue that were now scattered like confetti amongst the hairs on his chest—"there's only one person he really wants, and that's you . . . I reckon there's only one person he's *ever* wanted, and it's always been you. So if he did happen to forget himself on just the one occasion and make a pass at you—"

"Well, he didn't!" And much Nicky would care even if he had. *He* plainly wouldn't be torn apart by pangs of jealousy. She pushed him away from her, snatching up her hairbrush and beating vigorously at her hair with it. "At least if he did," she said, "it would make a change . . . at least it would show *some*one didn't think I was just a bag of old chicken bones."

The blue eyes widened.

"Hell's bells! You're surely not holding *that* against me? It was only meant as a joke."

"Oh. Was it?" she said.

"Of course it was, you daft trollop!"

"You don't behave as if it was."

"What do you mean, I don't behave as if it was?"

"I mean *you* quite obviously have no inclination to make a pass at me!"

There was a short silence, then Nicky laughed—but a trifle uncertainly, a trifle embarrassed. It had not his usual ring of confidence.

"I never knew you wanted me to make a pass at you! *Do* you want me to make a pass at you?"

She wished with all her heart that she

could say no, but the tears were running so fast down her cheeks she couldn't say anything at all. She just sat there, weeping, with her hair brush in her hands.

"Well, hell, if I'd *known*," said Nicky. He stood looking down at her, as if for once in his life at a loss what to do. "You should have told me, or something. I mean—" He ran a hand through his hair. "How was I to guess?"

"It's all right." She wiped the back of her hand across her nose. "You don't have to apologize. I know I'm n-not what you'd c-call exactly s-*sexy*—"

"Who says you're not?" He squatted on his heels beside her, grinning hopefully in an effort to make her smile. "Course you are! Here—" he thrust a fresh handful of tissues at her. "Sexiest thing on two legs! What's the matter? You think I'm just saying it?"

"I know p-perfectly well you're just s-saying it!" She mopped at her eyes with the tissues. Despite herself, a reluctant watery smile was already teasing up the corners of her mouth. "If it were true you wouldn't have needed to be told . . . you'd have thought of it for yourself!"

"Oh, I would, would I? All right, then . . . all right! If that's the way you want it—" He suddenly took her hands in his and pulled her to her feet. "I'll show you whether it's true or not . . . come on! Don't be bashful!" He jerked her towards the bed. "You've asked for it, my girl— now you're going to get it! And you needn't try shouting rape, because there isn't anyone to hear you . . ."

She had not the least inclination to try shouting rape. Nicky was at liberty to do with her just whatever he chose, as he must surely always have known, had he ever stopped to think. Obviously he never had. *You should have told me or something* . . . Perhaps he was right. Perhaps she should have done. It had not been as difficult as all that, and at least when she had he had responded—unlike Alex, for all he was reputed to be some kind of a cross between Rudolph Valentino and Casanova. Whether such illustrious heritage could also have been claimed for Nicky she could not have said, for she had no means of comparison, and neither did she care. Whether he were good lover or bad, it mattered not to her. It was enough only that he was Nicky—even if he had soaked himself in her Yves St. Laurent, even if his beard did scrape her cheek and make it sore. She would rather a thousand times it was scraping hers than someone else's.

"There you are, you see!" He raised himself on one elbow, laughing down at her. "What did I tell you? Sexiest thing on two legs—didn't I just prove it to you? Couldn't do that if you didn't turn me on, now, could I?"

"I suppose not," she said, with humble gratitude.

"You bet your life not! That Danielle . . . no way. Doesn't do a thing to me. But a bag of old chicken bones—" He ruffled her hair. "Don't worry, kiddo. For a bag of old bones, you're not so bad!"

Coming from Nicky, it could only be

taken as a compliment. He rolled over on to his side. For a few blissful moments he lay there, quietly, idly stroking a finger down her cheek where his chin had scraped it; then: "Hang on a minute," he said. With one athletic bound he was back on his feet and across to the door. "You stay where you are, I'll be right back."

The door closed behind him. There was a second's pause, then she heard the unmistakable click of the telephone receiver being removed from its rest. Of course—he was going out. She had almost forgotten. He had been pressing his trousers, wondering whether or not to shave. She sat up. She could hear him dialling a number—impossible not to wonder which number it was. Softly she padded across to the door. Silence. The telephone would be ringing at the other end. Then there came Nicky's voice: "Trudi? That you?"

Her cheeks flared scarlet. She took a dive back into bed, pulled the covers up round her ears. Eavesdropping on Nicky! How could she? All he had been doing was telephoning Vic and Trudi. She couldn't possibly be jealous of Trudi— not *Trudi*. Nicky could have his pick of the bunch. He wouldn't pick someone old enough to be his mother—and anyway, Trudi belonged to Vic, and Vic was his friend. He wouldn't play that sort of mean trick on a friend.

He reappeared in the doorway.

"Right," he said. "That's that. Now— what do you feel like doing?"

She ought to have rejoiced. He had made love to her, he had cancelled whatever else he had had planned, he was obviously intending to devote the rest of his evening to her—and all she could feel was a deep emptiness and sense of desolation. Nicky sat himself down on the bed beside her.

"So what do you want to do?"

His tone was gentle enough: why, then, all the self-pity? All the despair? Whence this almost overwhelming desire to put her head beneath the pillow and weep?

"Mm?"

He was leaning over her, trying to coax

her. If he would only climb back into bed and take her in his arms and kiss her and hold her and tell her that he loved her.

"There's a film on down the road about vampires." He brushed a strand of hair off her cheek. "Want to come and see it? I'll buy you a bag of peanuts and we can sit and hold hands in the back row."

"I think I'd rather go and have a drink." Go and have several drinks. Why not? "Let's take a cab and go over to the Hereford and play darts like we used to."

That had been when she first joined the Company—when Nicky was still living at home. Life had been so easy, then. So untroubled, so uncomplicated. There had been none of this tearing jealousy, no constant ache at her heart.

Nicky shook his head.

"Can't go to the Hereford. Go across to the Cedars, if you like, have a game there."

"I don't want to go across to the Cedars! I want to go back to the Hereford." She wanted to be happy again, wanted to relive old times. "Why can't we go there? What's the matter with it?"

"Been taken over—new clientele. Alexis wouldn't approve."

"If you mean it's full of prostitutes, it always was."

"Yeah, but they were the female sort. It's gone the other way now. Be as much as my reputation's worth to show my face in there with you in tow—wearing that gear?" He nodded his head towards her discarded sweater and jeans. "Be asking for trouble—be like it was in Istanbul. You needn't think I'm going to forget *that* in a hurry. Dragging me into some sleazy dive in some sleazy back street . . . *Oh, really. Nicky, don't be such a prude, Nicky, nothing's going to HAPPEN, Nicky* . . . oh, no! We only find ourselves half mobbed, that's all . . . *Would your little brother like to buy a radio*, for heaven's sake! Never mind trying to flog us stolen radios—never mind all the hash and the pot and the dirty magazines—never even mind some lubricious old Turk actually trying to *buy* you off me,

it's the little brother bit that gets me . . .
little brother! Like hell! They didn't
think you were my *little brother*, they—"
He stopped. "*Now* what's the matter?
Now what am I supposed to have done?"

She choked, and scrubbed at her eyes
with the edge of the sheet.

"You don't have to keep going on
about it!"

"Going on about it? That's the first
time I've mentioned it!"

"About *me*—the fact that I'm just a
b-bag of old ch-chicken b-bones!"

"For crying out loud! Don't say you're
going to get all hung up about it? If it
makes you any happier, I *like* my women
that way . . . I *like* 'em skinny. I *like* 'em
to be mistaken for my little brother. I—"

"That's not what you said before!"

"So haven't I just *proved* it? You're
fine the way you are. Come on, now! I
never knew such a waterspout. Stop
howling and tell me what you want to
do."

"I told you . . . I want to go to the
Hereford and play darts."

"And I told you, you can't."

"Why not?" She pushed her hair back over her ears in a defiant gesture. "I don't *have* to wear jeans. I don't *have* to be taken for your little brother—since you seem so sensitive on the point."

"Me? *I'm* not the one who's sensitive —you are! You're the one who keeps bursting into tears all over the place. It doesn't bother me one way or the other. They can think what they like, as far as I'm concerned."

"All right, so what's all the fuss about? Why can't we go? We—"

"Look!" Nicky stood up. "I'm not taking you there. That's it. *Finis.* All there is to it. You want to go, you go with someone else; not me. Got it? Right. Now —we either go across to the Cedars and we play darts, or we go down the road and we see a film about vampires. Which is it to be?"

There was no point in arguing with him: she chose the vampires. She tried comforting herself with the reflection that she didn't really mind what they did, so long as they could do it together. Even vampires became something of a special treat, with Nicky at her side.

5

THE new season was opening on a Wednesday at the start of November with a performance of *Sleeping Beauty. Adam* was to have its first night shortly before Christmas—still well over a month away, but drawing uncomfortably closer with every day that passed. Never in her life had Gill felt so unhappy with a part. Vaingloriously had she boasted to Kath that "that was different, that was dancing": *I can do anything if I can DANCE it*—but not, it seemed, the rôle of Temptation. It eluded her even yet. She could scarcely any longer lay the blame at Nicky's door. He had done as much as any man could reasonably be expected to do. If after *that* she had no confidence, the fault could be only with her.

They had been a strange, unsettling few days that had passed since Nicky had made love to her. The very first occasion on which he had done it he had behaved afterwards as if nothing had occurred: their relationship had continued just the same as it had always been. Now he seemed oddly disturbed and ill at ease, almost as if he felt guilty at having done it at all. He was quite obviously uncertain how to treat her, and she, for want of any cue, was far too shy to prompt. He was gentler with her than he was in the habit of being, but she felt it was the gentleness of concern, more of a brotherly benevolence than a lover's tenderness.

He made no attempt to repeat his performance of Sunday, though for four days he stayed at home in the evenings, not even suggesting they go up the road for a drink or see more films about vampires, but simply turning on the television and slumping himself in an armchair before it until bedtime. It was possible that for once he was quite genuinely weary, for the run-up to opening night was always strenuous, what with final rehearsals of this and technical run-throughs of that—what with costume rehearsals and lighting rehearsals, what with photo calls and orchestra calls and Madame scurrying about like a hen without its head and no one ever knowing from one minute to the next when they were going to find themselves suddenly scheduled for an extra couple of hours in the studio "just to put the final touches", "just to make quite sure", "just to smooth those ragged edges". Not even Nicky's supply of energy could be inexhaustible: even he, from time to time, must call a halt.

For four nights he had stayed in, and then, on Friday evening, the telephone had rung. It had rung on other evenings, and each time that it had Nicky had leapt across the room like a scalded cat and snatched at the receiver. This time, because he was outside in the kitchen and she was right on top of it, Gill had been the one to answer. At the other end of the line, a female voice had asked for Nicky. It was a voice with a quite strongly marked German accent, but it wasn't

Trudi. She would have recognized Trudi, and in any case Trudi would have said hello to her. This one, with grave Teutonic formality, said only: "Good evening. May I speak please, if he is there, with Nicky one moment?"

Nicky had been there almost immediately. He had appeared at Gill's elbow with a tea towel in one hand, a fish slice in the other.

"Who is it? Is it for me? The rice is nearly boiling, by the way."

She had handed over the receiver, relieved him of the tea towel and the fish slice, gone out to the kitchen to take over the cooking of the evening meal—which Nicky for once had offered to do by himself.

"You go and sit down, put your feet up, have a drink . . . I'll see to it. You just leave it to me."

In the event, it had been Gill who had seen to it. Not that Nicky had been on the telephone for any length of time— indeed, she had heard the click of the receiver being replaced in its cradle barely seconds after she had prevented the rice from boiling over; but from that point on he had seemed to lose all interest in the preparation of dinner, even to the extent of forgetting that he had ever offered to "see to it" in the first place. When she went back through to the sitting room she found him standing at the windows, forehead pressed against the glass. He hadn't looked up as she came in—had perhaps not even been aware of her presence. She hadn't liked to ask him what was wrong: somehow, whatever it was, she had felt that she would rather not know. When he finally came back out to the kitchen and awkwardly, with a note of apology in his voice, said: "Gilly, I—I'm afraid I'm going to have to go out tonight after all," she had not been surprised. She had known, then, that it was not tiredness had kept him at home the past few days but a sense of obligation towards *her*. She had never wanted Nicky to feel obliged. The last thing she had ever intended was to be a drag on him. She had managed to give a little laugh and say: "*I*'m not your keeper . . . it's Madame you'll have to answer to, not me, when you nod off in the middle of rehearsal!"

The laugh had plainly done nothing to convince. Before leaving, he had not only insisted on helping her with the washing up, despite her assurances that there was no need (for what, after all, had *she* to do for the rest of the evening?) but had even gone so far as to switch on the television in a vain attempt to find something on one of the channels that might keep her amused for an hour or two. His efforts were touching, but misplaced. Stoicism in the face of indifference is relatively easy: stoicism in the face of all too obvious concern becomes well nigh impossible. His hopeful "Be all right?" as he opened the front door, coupled as it was with a quick hug and a kiss and a parting "I won't be back too late, honest," had very nearly proved her undoing. After some hesitation, when he had gone, she had tried ringing Alex—only the sound of his voice, with its cheerful Cockney vowel sounds and the Hs none too certain even now, would have been of comfort to her. Alas, Alex also had been out (doing things with Danielle, no doubt). For once even he had failed her.

She had been in bed when Nicky arrived back. He had been true to his promise: it was barely on midnight. She had heard the front door open and close, heard his footsteps along the passage—heard them stop outside her door; then: "Gilly?" The door had opened a crack and Nicky's head had appeared round it. There was just sufficient light from the passage for her to see him by. "You awake?"

She had managed to say "Yes" in tones that were reasonably normal: she could only hope that he wouldn't switch on the light. He hadn't.

"Just thought I'd look in," he said, "and let you know I was back."

She had made a muffled noise into the sheet. Nicky had hesitated.

"Want anything to drink?"

Another muffled noise.

"No? Well—see you in the morning, then. Night night."

Her eyes when she opened them next day had been quite swollen and heavy-lidded. She had had to use a liberal amount of green-frosted eye shadow in order to disguise the fact, and then, because green-frosted eye shadow went somewhat ill with blue denims, had had to dress herself up in her best black trousers and a silk blouse to go with them. Nicky, in his usual morning uniform of ragged sweater and frayed jeans, with his hair uncombed and his chin unshaven, had taken one look at her across the breakfast table and said: "Get her! What's all the campery in aid of? Got your mink leotard on as well, have you? Be asking me to walk on the other side of the road next . . ."

For all his teasing, she felt that he had guessed at the truth behind those green-frosted eyes. He held her hand quite firmly in his all the way to the theatre, which was something he almost never did, or only very casually, and in the studio, before all the Company, as they waited for class to begin, he put his arms round her and said: "Hello, skinbag . . . I love yer!" It was the first time he had ever seen fit to tell her so; but instead of bursting with joy her heart only contracted still further with misery. She didn't want to be loved merely as a consolation prize—she didn't want to be loved out of duty or of pity. She wanted Nicky to love her the way that she loved him, unsparingly, unflinchingly, to the exclusion of all else that the world might hold. It was something which she knew, deep inside herself, he never would.

Class ended that morning at half-past eleven. Gill, not called back until the evening, when they had the final run-through of *Sleeping Beauty* before the dress rehearsal on Monday, found herself free for the rest of the day. Nicky, she knew, was going to be involved for most of the afternoon working with Derek and Alex on the death of Mercutio scene from *Romeo & Juliet*. Nicky was a natural for Mercutio, just as Alex was for Romeo—

just as she herself was for Juliet. One day she would dance the part; but it wouldn't be with Nicky.

She had a quick cup of coffee with Kath, who now that she had decided to burn her boats was full of wedding plans and already talking excitedly of bridesmaids' dresses and where to go for a honeymoon, and went back by herself to Guilford Street. The post had come: two brown envelopes which looked like bills, plus a card for Nicky. The card was from Germany, from Vic and Trudi. In Vic's big bold scrawl it said: *Best of luck opening night, see you soon, love to Gill, Vic & Trudi*. They must be on holiday. Nicky, of course, would never have thought to mention it. She was glad, at any rate, that Vic had remembered her.

She went through to the kitchen, did the washing up from breakfast, had another cup of coffee, looked at her watch: half-past one. She should have asked Kath round for the afternoon, except that Kath could talk of nothing but weddings. It was natural enough, she supposed, but she really wasn't in the mood for it just at present.

She decided, for want of anything better to do, that she might as well take the opportunity to ransack Nicky's drawers and see what mending had accumulated. There was nothing more conducive to morbid melancholy and self-pity as sitting about doing nothing. She unearthed three sweaters with holes at the elbows and a shirt with two buttons missing. That should be enough to keep her busy for a good half of the afternoon. By then it would be time to have a bath and think of returning to the theatre. As she crossed back to the door, something on the bedside table caught her eye. It was a pencil sketch, head and shoulders, done on a sheet of rough card which looked as if it might have been torn from a cereal packet. It was, quite unmistak-ably, Nicky. Whoever had been respon-sible for it had caught him to perfection. She stood a moment, looking down at it, wondering why he had never thought to show it to her. He must have known she would be interested. It really was a quite extraordinary likeness. In one corner was a signature, but study it closely though she might she was unable to decipher it. She made a mental note to ask Nicky that evening. It was, after all, only natural that her curiosity should be roused: he could scarcely object to *that*.

She had just settled down with her mending when the telephone rang. She went out to the hall to answer it.

"Hello?"

"Hello . . . May I speak with Nicky again one moment if he is there, please?"

It was the same girl who had rung before—the girl who had taken him away from her: the girl who had induced him to change his mind at the last minute. *I'm afraid I'm going to have to go out after all* . . . She said, rather coldly:

"He's not here. He's at the theatre."

"Ah . . . Do you know when he will be free maybe?"

"I should think at about midnight, or possibly even later."

"*Oh, ja! Natürlich!* He has the dress rehearsal, no?"

"A run-through. Yes. They usually go on until the small hours. Do you want me to give him a message?"

"Well—" Did she sense some slight hesitation? Some reluctance, perhaps, to entrust her with so important a task? "Well, that would be very kind in you . . . I am ringing only to say that we have here his—how do you call it? *Brieftasche* . . . wallet! This is it. It is containing his motor licence and his bank card. I am thinking maybe he will be missing it and not knowing."

And just how was *she* knowing? Motor licence and bank card, indeed! What right had she, whoever she was, to go poking round amongst the contents of his wallet? And how could Nicky possibly have *left* his wallet? Careless he was, but surely not that careless? Unless—She tried hard to think back to what he had been wearing last night. Jacket? Or only sweater? If he'd had a jacket, then the wallet would have been in the inside pocket and might

149

just conceivably have fallen out if at any time he had taken it off. If on the other hand he'd had only a sweater, then presumably the wallet, in his usual haphazard fashion, would have been stuck in the back pocket of his jeans, and—

"I'll tell him," she said. "Who shall I say rang?"

"If you will say to him that it is Gundi—"

"Gundi?"

"Gundi, *ja*. From *Die Drei Sterne*."

The *Drei Sterne*—the Three Stars. That was Vic and Trudi's place. But Vic and Trudi weren't there—Vic and Trudi were on holiday in Germany. He had gone there last night to see this Gundi. (Gundi! Ridiculous name!) He had gone there and he had left his wallet there and now the woman was actually ringing up to tell *her* —well, all right, then. She banged down the receiver. Since she was the one who had been told about it, she would be the one to go and pick it up. She would go out to Chalk Farm and she would collect it for him in person. She would take a look at this Gundi whom he seemed to find such an attraction.

They had been working on the Mercutio-Tybalt scene for the better part of two hours. Even Nicky for once had no objections to make when Alex suggested they call it a day. Nicky in fact had been surprisingly subdued throughout the whole session. There had been none of his usual ebullience, none of his usual inspired clowning. Now, as Alex prepared to follow Derek through the door, he found himself held back by Nicky's hand on his arm.

"Alex—"

He turned.

"Yup?"

"Any chance of a quick word?"

"Sure. Go ahead. What's eating you?"

Nicky hesitated. He seemed, for Nicky, quite strangely at a loss.

"I—" He waved a hand. "I just wanted—"

"Just wanted—?"

"Just wanted to—to ask you—"

Again he broke off. Alex looked down at him. It was no new thing to have Nicky turn to him in a moment of crisis—that, after all, was what he was there for. Had he not promised Gill's mother, only hours before she died, that he would always take care of both of them, of Nicky as well as of Gill? Nicky's life since then had been full of crises of one kind or another, but never before had he known the boy so tongue-tied, so obviously ill at ease. Far more like Nicky to blurt everything out pell mell just as it came. If he were having difficulty, then it could only be something serious.

"Look, whatever it is," he said, "whatever daft thing you've gone and done—"

Nicky smiled, faintly and sardonically.

"It's nothing I've *done*—more like just the opposite. More like something I haven't done."

"Oh? Well, that makes a change, anyway!" A thought suddenly struck him. "It wouldn't be anything to do with Gill, would it?" He knew at once, from the guarded expression which passed across

Nicky's face, that that was exactly what it was to do with. "You and Gill?" Of course, he should have guessed. He had been half expecting something of the sort ever since last Sunday. "So what's the trouble?" he said.

There was a silence. Nicky hunched a shoulder.

"Well, come on," said Alex. "Let's be having it. You might just as well tell me now you've started . . . What, exactly, is the problem?"

The *Drei Sterne*, at two o'clock in the afternoon, was virtually deserted: only a pair of old ladies drinking coffee in a corner and a boy behind the bar desultorily pushing cocktail sticks into cherries. The place had been done up since the one and only time that Gill had been there. The walls had been painted deep crimson and decorated with bold ceramic murals in vivid mauves and greens and bright electric blue. What precisely they were supposed to represent —if indeed anything at all—she could not have said, but certainly they had a curious fascination about them. She found herself almost compelled to go up and touch one, and had sternly to resist the impulse. She had not come here for a living art session with bits of coloured pottery, she had come here on business.

"Excuse me—"

The boy with the cocktail sticks looked up as she approached. He had black hair and an olive skin and big brown eyes like a fawn. He struck her, she couldn't quite have said why, as being not quite all there. When she asked him about the wallet and said that someone called Gundi had just rung, he reacted like a startled rabbit, giving her a frightened, big-eyed stare, then turning tail and diving out through the swing doors at the back of the counter without so much as a word. Gill was left standing there, alone but for the two old ladies. She wondered if the boy were simple, or only foreign.

The swing doors were pushed open again; a girl came through. She was tall and very blonde, blonder even than Alex, almost flaxen. Her eyes were wide and clear grey-blue, her face a model of perfect bone structure. She was wearing a dress of some slinky, silky, shiny material that clung to the contours of her body and emphasized the deep ripe fullness of the breasts and the slight curve of the stomach. Her hips, for all her long-legged slenderness, were quite definitely feminine. Certainly no danger of anyone mistaking *her* for Nicky's little brother. She smiled a friendly smile: it seemed guileless enough.

"You are asking for me?"

Hadn't she just said that she was? Hadn't she just explained the whole purpose of her mission to the olive-skinned boy with the liquid brown eyes?

"You rang me," she said. "About Nicky's wallet—"

"Ah!" That settled it. The boy was obviously a simpleton. If he couldn't even pass on a straightforward message—"You must be Gillian, *ja?* I am Gundi." She held out a hand. It was warm and shapely, and eminently capable. "How do you do? I am so very pleased to be meeting you in the end. Nicky is telling us always so much of you. You and—Alexis, is it not? We are hearing all the time of you. I think he is very fond of you both, no? Gino—" She turned to the boy, who had followed her back out and was engaged once again with his cocktail sticks and his cherries, though Gill was perfectly well aware that he was covertly studying her from under the soot-black lashes. "Gino, this lady—" she spoke very slowly and carefully, as if to an idiot child. Assuredly the boy was not quite right in the head—"this lady is coming for Nicky's wallet. Could you fetch it for us, please . . . the wallet—with the money." Graphically she mimed both wallet and money. "*Comprende?*"

The boy nodded. As he went out again through the swing door, he shot Gill a curious glance over his shoulder. She had the feeling that even he, slow on the uptake though he plainly was, knew exactly what was going on between Nicky and this cool, self-possessed German girl, with her air of patronizing friendship, her regal *I am so pleased to be meeting you in the end*. Of course, she could afford to be patronizing: she could afford to be regal. After last night she must feel herself very secure. Doubtless it would have been a rather different tale if Nicky had chosen to remain at home with Gill. But Nicky hadn't. He had chosen to come round here and spend his evening with Gundi and leave his wallet behind.

"Gino will get it for us." The woman smiled again; the free, frank, open smile of victor over vanquished. "You will take a coffee, *ja? Aber ja!* I insist . . . when you are coming all this way just for the *böse* Nicky, because he is so *stumm*—I am thinking he should be more careful with his things, no? I am telling to him before about this. I am saying to him, one day, my *Liebling*, you will be forgetting your head . . . he is like this at home, perhaps? I think to be living with this boy you are having to be a little bit of an angel, *nicht wahr?* How long now since you are putting up with him?"

"If you mean sharing the flat," said Gill, "only about a year. If you mean actually living with him—"

"Ah, but not!" Gundi gave a merry Germanic laugh. "This of a certainty I am not meaning! *To live with* . . . this is to say, to be lovers with, I think, *auf Englisch?* At school I am learning it as something different, but since I am to England coming I am finding much double meaning. Nicky is sometimes teaching to me what I think are naughty words. He is saying things and then when I am repeating them Vic is growing quite mad and Trudi she is laughing, and all the peoples they are pulling at my leg— but I think this is Nicky, no? He is— how do you say? Funny boy. Always he is making us to laugh. We are all loving him very much."

Yes, thought Gill; I'm sure you are. This was a whole area of Nicky's life that was quite unknown to her. She didn't want to hear about it—not, at any rate, from cool blonde German girls with blue eyes and long legs and deep, full breasts that made a sad mockery of her own matchstick frailty. *That's the trouble with all you little sylphlike creatures . . .*

Gino came back with Nicky's wallet. He held it out to her without speaking. She took it and thanked him, but still he didn't say anything; only subjected her to yet another of his solemn big-eyed stares and went back to his cocktail sticks. Really he would have been quite exceptionally handsome were it not for that curious vacancy of expression. Nicky should have taken the time to teach *him* a few naughty words while he was about it. Might have livened the boy up a bit. But of course, with Gundi about the place he wouldn't have eyes to spare for anyone else. Gundi came across to the door with her. Her last words were:

"You will tell to Nicky, please . . . he is promising the tickets for the ballet. You will say to him not to forget?"

"It's not that I don't care about her: I do care about her. I care about her desperately. That's the very reason I've come to you—yes, and you don't have to look at me like that! Just because—because *this* has happened—it doesn't mean to say I'm happy about having to hurt her. You think it doesn't bother me, how she's going to feel? You think I haven't spent the last few weeks wondering what the hell I'm going to do about it? I do *love* her, you know—I love her every bit as much as you do."

Alex smiled, rather wryly. *I doubt that*, he thought. *I doubt that very much* . . . Aloud, he said:

"You just happen to have a funny way of showing it."

"Oh, come off it, Alex! So I love her one way, you love her another way—look, I'm not blind: I do *know* how you feel about her. *She* may not, but *I* do. So all right . . . all right! Maybe I don't love her *that* way—but I can still care about her, can't I? I can still care what *happens* to her."

"It strikes me," Alex could not help saying, a trifle drily, "that if you really cared as much as all that—"

"I wouldn't have got myself into this position?"

"Well—would you?"

"How the hell do I know whether I would or not? Maybe I would, maybe I wouldn't. It's not something you plan in advance. In any case, I'm not a saint, for God's sakes! I've got just the same faults and failings as anyone else, I—" Nicky stopped. "Yes, yes . . . very funny. You had realized. So OK, what am I supposed to do? Live on top of a pole? I haven't noticed you exactly being celibate."

"There is, however, a slight difference, wouldn't you say?"

Nicky flushed.

"Well, of course, if you're going to start coming all moral on me—"

"Oh, don't be a damned little fool! I'm not coming all moral on you. What you do is your own affair—except when it happens to concern Gill. What beats me is why in God's name you ever encouraged her to move in with you in the first place."

"I wouldn't have done," said Nicky, "if I'd realized."

"Realized what? That you—"

"No. I mean about her."

"You're not seriously trying to stand there and tell me you never *realized* the way that girl felt about you?"

"Not until it was too late."

Alex looked at him, rather hard.

"Well, all right! All right! So I knew she had a thing about me—like I can twist her round my little finger any time I want . . . like if I let her she'd lie down on the carpet and let me walk all over her. But I swear to God I never realized she felt like *this*. I thought it was more —well, you know . . . kid sister stuff. That's why I said OK—move in, share the flat. Why not? *I* didn't know."

"*You* didn't know . . . everybody else did, but not you—and you think you're not blind? You're as blind as a flaming bat! For crying out loud! What the hell did you think was going to happen? I suppose you imagined you could carry on just exactly the same as usual? Just carry on amusing yourself the same as if she wasn't there? *She* wouldn't mind. She had her life to lead, you had yours . . . Jesus wept! It's no bloody wonder the poor kid's got herself all screwed up. How was *she* to know? That's more to the point, isn't it? There she is, eating her heart out, and you not taking a damned bit of notice—"

"I took notice! What are you talking about? Of course I took notice!"

"Oh, yes, I'm sure you did . . . held her hand occasionally, patted her on the cheek, told her what a good girl she was, all that kind of thing?"

"A bit more than that," said Nicky. "A little bit more than that."

"I hope you're not implying that you were actually crass enough to try taking her to bed with you? After all you've just told me—you actually did *that?*" Alex stared down, exasperated. "Just what is wrong with you? Have you got no sense of responsibility at *all?* I thought you said you cared about that girl?"

"I do care about her! Why else do you

think I did it? I did it because she wanted me to—because even I, in my batlike blindness, believe it or not, was capable of seeing *that*."

"Holy mother of God!"

Alex turned away in disgust. Nicky's flush deepened.

"So what's so wrong with it?"

"Just about everything, you half-baked lout! You really thought *that* was going to solve anything? For her *or* for you?"

Nicky shifted his feet.

"I just couldn't stand seeing her unhappy."

"No? Well, you're going to see her a damned sight more unhappy now, aren't you? After all these years, you can still be that naïve? It never occurred to you, I suppose, that doing a thing like that might just conceivably make the situation even worse than it already was?"

"So what would you have done?"

"I?" Alex curled his lip, contemptuously. "I like to think that I would have resisted the temptation . . . and if *I* could resist it—"

"Yes, all right! You don't have to spell it out. So maybe I made a mistake."

"So maybe you made one hell of a lot of mistakes!"

"Well, don't get mad at me, just tell me what we're going to do."

"What *we're* going to do?"

"Oh, Alexis, be an angel—" Nicky, with sudden change of tactic, slid both arms round Alex's neck and looked up at him, entreatingly. "Help me out of this and I'll never ask you to do anything for me ever again."

That, too, was something he very much doubted. Firmly, he extricated himself from Nicky's embrace.

"And just what sort of magic wand am *I* supposed to be able to wave?"

"You could—talk to her."

"You mean I could break it to her?"

"Yes. You could break it to her. You could explain to her. How it happened— how I never realized. Tell her that I love her—because I do, I swear to you I do!"

"So why not go and tell her yourself?

165

Why waste your breath telling me? I'm not the one you've got to convince."

"But you're the one that could convince her . . . Look, I just don't want her being *hurt* at all. I just don't want her thinking that I don't *care* . . . oh, come on, Alex! Have a heart! How can *I* break it to her?"

"The same way you've broken it to me, I would imagine."

"Alex, please . . . please! I'm asking you . . . just this once . . . help me!"

It was never easy to harden one's heart against a really impassioned appeal from Nicky, but for once, for just this once, he managed it. There was almost nothing he wouldn't do for the boy, but he wasn't doing this. Nicky had got himself into this mess, it was up to him to get himself out of it again. Not even for him was he prepared to be the ambassador with this sort of news. *He does love you REALLY* —for heaven's sakes! What kind of comfort was that supposed to be? What solace was that going to bring to one who loved as passionately, as all-embracingly, as Gill?

"Nicky, I'm sorry," he said. "This is one case where I can't be of any assistance. You're just going to have to take a long, deep breath and break it to her yourself—and make very sure, when you do, that you do it gently."

Nicky was in his dressing-room when Gill arrived back at the theatre. She tossed his wallet across to him.

"Here! In case you might be needing it."

He seemed surprised.

"Where did you find it?"

"Where you left it."

"I didn't even know that I *had* left it. Where was it? In my bedroom?"

"No." It was all she could do not to say, *in someone else's bedroom* . . . "At Vic and Trudi's. A girl rang up. I thought I might as well go and get it for you."

"Oh." He swallowed. "Well—thank you."

"That's all right. I didn't have anything else to do."

There was a pause. Nicky stood with

the wallet in his hands, Gill stood watching him. They both opened their mouths to speak at the same time.

"She's—"

"Gill—"

Another pause.

"Well—" Nicky laughed, a little awkwardly. "That's saved me a trip, anyway."

Carelessly, he stuffed the wallet into the back pocket of his trousers.

"I see they've changed the décor," said Gill.

"Oh?"

"Since the last time I was there . . . all those exotic murals."

"Oh, yes. Quite fun, aren't they?"

"If you like that kind of thing." Why did she have to be so ungracious? Just because she hated the whole place and everything in it—"Who's the half-witted boy behind the bar?"

Nicky frowned slightly.

"He's not half-witted. He's deaf and dumb."

"Oh." She wondered, for a moment, if

she felt ashamed, and then decided that she didn't. After all, no one had told her. How could she be expected to know? If Nicky would never take her anywhere, would never introduce her to anyone—"I hadn't noticed," she said. "I didn't really get much chance. Your friend Gundi's quite a talker, isn't she?"

Nicky turned. He held out a hand towards her.

"Gilly, I—"

Whatever it was, she didn't want to hear. She tore open the door.

"I'd better be getting a move on. It's nearly quarter to. Just keep your fingers crossed we're through by midnight—oh, and before I forget." She put her head back through the door. "Don't wait for me afterwards . . . I'm going home with Alex."

"Going home with Alex?"

"He said he'd give me a lift."

"You're going back to Clapham?"

"Just for the weekend. I—I thought it would make a change."

"Ah."

"There are things I want to do—want to get sorted out."

"Yes. Well—good idea." He winked at her. "Dirty weekend with Alexis, eh? You just keep an eye on that boyo. I told you before . . . he's not to be trusted!"

6

"YOU should have let me know sooner what your plans were—I could have put things off till next Sunday. I don't like going out and leaving you here by yourself all day."

"Don't be so silly," said Gill. "I shan't be here by myself—there's always Nanty, isn't there? I might even do my duty and go and sit with her for a bit. And anyway—"

And anyway, she didn't want Alex putting Danielle off just for her; not a second time. She had already had Nicky staying indoors four nights on the trot only because he felt himself obliged to do so, she wasn't having Alex make the same sacrifice.

"Anyway," she said, firmly, "I've got things to do."

"I see! You mean I should be in your way?"

"Exactly. So off you go and enjoy yourself with Danielle—" she picked up his car keys, pushed them into his hand, chivvied him before her to the front door —"and I'll see you in the morning."

"Oh, before that," he said. "Long before that. We should be back by ten at the very latest."

"All right," she said. "I'll see you then . . . have a good day."

She felt at a loss when Alex had gone. It was true enough she had "things to do" —but they were mental things, not physical. She scarcely even knew where to begin. You couldn't sit down and sort out your emotional problems with the same ease as you could sit down and tidy your desk drawers or tackle a pile of mending. You couldn't really sit down and sort them out at all; but that, somehow, was what she had to do. Kath had been quite right: one couldn't go on indefinitely.

She sat for most of the afternoon with Nanty, who was in one of her less objectionable moods. She even risked food poisoning by taking tea with her—she even let the cat sit on her lap as she did so. She tried pretending to herself that this had been the sole, benevolent purpose of her visit, to do her duty by seeing Nanty; but she knew that it wasn't. She was only prolonging the hour when she must apply her mind to some hard, objective thinking.

At four o'clock she went out to look at the garden, but it was growing dark already and even if it hadn't been she would have had not the least idea what needed doing. She ran a bath, instead, and stayed in there with the radio for company until the water grew cold and it was warmer out than in. In her bedroom, which was still kept just the same as it had always been, even though she wasn't living there any more, she maundered a while amongst her old childhood possessions, the ballet books, the albums, the signed photograph of Fonteyn, indulged in a few memories, knew, still, that she was but postponing the hour of reckoning, went out to the kitchen to see what Alex kept in the cupboards. He kept very little. Like most men by themselves, he plainly was not much of a housekeeper. She helped herself to a can of soup and a tin of baked beans and took them through to the sitting-room. For two hours she watched the television, but could scarcely have told what it was that she saw. At eight o'clock, with the sudden impatience of despair, she switched it off. What was to be gained from sitting here all evening if tomorrow she were to return to the very same situation as the one she had left? There was only one solution to her problem, and that was to face up to it. To pluck up the courage to go to Nicky and to ask him outright. *This Gundi . . . is she just someone to amuse yourself with or is it really serious?* If he said no, it was nothing, then she would pluck up her courage still further and tell him exactly why it mattered to her so desperately. If on the other hand he said yes, it really was serious—well, at least she would know where she stood. Whatever the answer was, she couldn't go on like this any more.

Having made up her mind, she knew that she must do it immediately. It was no use waiting until tomorrow, for her courage would surely fail. She would only find herself back again with her head in the sand and her fingers stuffed determinedly into her ears. It must be now or not at all. She re-packed her bag, left a note for Alex—*Changed mind, went back to flat after all. See you in class*—was about to leave the house when it rather belatedly occurred to her that at ten minutes past eight on a Sunday evening Nicky was not very likely to be at home. Pointless returning to an empty flat and having to wait until two or three o'clock in the morning for him. She went back along the hall to the telephone, rang the Guilford Street number—and was so surprised when Nicky's voice at the other end said "Hello?" that in a moment of foolish panic she put back the receiver without saying anything at all. Had she secretly been banking on his not being there? Was that to have been her cowardly let-out? If so, she had spiked her own guns, for with Nicky at home she was left with no alternative.

She took a cab from the nearest cab rank, was in Guilford Street within the half hour. As she paid off the driver, she saw that there was a light on in Nicky's bedroom. For the first time, the thought struck her: suppose he was not alone? Suppose he actually had *her* in there with him? The idea filled her with revulsion. Such a possibility had not before occurred to her. Now that it did, she knew a strong temptation to abandon her mission, to jump back into the cab and run away again without showing herself. It was only the fact that the cab was already moving off that stopped her. Resolutely, she forced herself to walk across the pavement, through the street door that was their own private entrance, up the three flights of uncarpeted stairs to the top. There she stopped. If he had *her* in there —but whether he did or he didn't it was too late to back out now. It would be altogether too faint-hearted to turn tail and disappear at this stage. She opened the front door, stepped through into the hall.

"Nicky, it's me, I'm—"

The words died on her lips. Nicky's bedroom opened directly off the hall. Not expecting her back, he had left the door gaping wide. She couldn't help seeing whether she would or not. She turned, precipitately, and fled. She heard Nicky's voice shout "Gilly!" from the top of the stairs, then again from his bedroom window. She took no notice but just went on running. His voice echoed after her down the street: "Gilly! For God's sake . . . come back!"

It was not quite nine o'clock when Alex arrived back with Danielle. He had been unable all day to rid his mind of thoughts of Gill. Why had she so suddenly decided on spending the weekend at home? She had not spent a weekend at home since the day she had moved in with Nicky. Was it something to do with the situation between them? Could Nicky at last have nerved himself to tell her what yesterday he had told Alex? It seemed hardly likely. He could scarcely yet have had the opportunity, and Gill, besides, would surely not be taking it so calmly? Not unless her feelings towards Nicky were rather different from what he had always supposed them to be. He called out to her as he opened the front door, but she did not reply. Upstairs, perhaps, with the old lady. He took Danielle through to the sitting-room.

"I'll just pop up and see if—"

Even as he spoke, the sheet of paper caught his eye. It was on the mantelshelf, propped against the clock. He took it down to read it: Danielle craned over his shoulder.

"Changed mind, went back to flat after all. See you in class . . . eh, bien! Per 'aps now we can repose ourselves." She twitched the paper away from him. "All zis fuss—'ow is it zat I put up wiz you?"

Laughing, she twined her arms about his neck, lips pouting provocatively, body pressed tight against his. In other moods it could scarcely have failed to elicit a response; this evening he found himself too concerned about Gill to be roused. Danielle and her charms left him, for the moment, quite cold. He would have dropped her off in Chelsea on their way back into town but that nine o'clock in the evening had struck even him, in his impatience, as a trifle early to be dumping her.

He disentangled himself.

"What do you mean, all this fuss?"

"I mean—" she grinned, wickedly, at him—"all zis fuss and *la petite Cendrililon n'est plus ici* . . . ze bird 'as flown ze nest. *Elle est revenue à son prince.*" And then, for his benefit: "Returned to 'er *méchant petit Nicky*. I sink it is as well 'e—" She broke off. "*Qu'est-ce que c'est ça?*"

"Sounds like someone coming in. Hang on." He went back into the hall. "Gill!" He stared at her, in surprise and consternation. "What are you doing here? I thought you'd—" Before he could finish, she had slammed the front door behind her and come hurtling towards him up the passage. The next second and she was in his arms, sobbing as if her heart would break. "Sweetheart, sweetheart," he said. "What is it? What's happened?" She didn't reply; just turned her head into his shoulder and went on weeping. "Hey, now!" He tilted her chin up. "Whatever it is, it can't be as bad as all that . . . come on! Give us a smile . . . tell us what the problem is. Not something to do with the two of you, is it? You and Nicky? Something he's said? Something he's done?" He knew from the convulsive way she clutched at him that he had guessed correctly. Not for the first time, he felt a strong desire to put his hands round Nicky's throat and choke the life out of him. *Gently*, he had said. *Break it to her gently* . . . Could that boy do *nothing* right? "Gilly—" He took his handkerchief from his pocket and coaxed it into her hand; then, bending his head, whispered: "Danielle's here . . . don't worry, I'll get rid of her. Go and dry your eyes, make us a cup of coffee. Be with you in a couple of secs. All right?"

In the sitting-room, Danielle said:

"I know, I know, you don' 'ave to tell me . . . two makes ze company, sree ze crowd. Already I am on my way."

He found himself feeling just the tiniest bit guilty.

"You won't mind if I don't run you back myself? I'll get you a cab, of course." God knows, it was the least he could do. "Don't tell me I'm behaving like a lout: I know it. I wouldn't normally ask it of you, but—"

"But *la petite Cendrillon est revenue* . . . ze bird is back in ze nest and you must go to 'er." She picked up her coat and held it out to him. Obediently, he took it. "Why does she cry so?"

"I don't know. That's what I'm aiming to find out."

"You don' suppose she 'as discovered, at last?"

"Discovered?" he said. "Discovered what?"

"*Mais la vérité, enfin!*

"What verity?"

"Why, about Nicky, of course!"

Of course? What did she mean, of course?

"I sink," said Danielle, "zat it was about time . . . *à vingt ans, alors, faut commencer à comprendre ces choses là. Peut pas rester toujours en état de petit enfant. T'es pas d'accord?*"

"No use asking me," he said.

He had told her before, she was wasting her breath addressing him in any other language than English. Not that he hadn't a fair suspicion of what she was talking about. At twenty years old, etc., etc.; and yes, it was perfectly true, one could not remain a child all one's life long. Gill would have had to learn the truth some time or other. Still, for all that, he had no intention of discussing the matter with Danielle.

"I'll go and ring for a cab," he said.

He turned on his heel and went back down the hall to the telephone. Danielle, nothing daunted, picked up her bag and followed him out.

"At first, even me, I do not mind to say zis to you, I am not knowing for sure . . . I sink one minute maybe, zen again maybe not . . . *enfin*, I am making ze leetle tests. Zen for sure I am knowing." She nodded her head, sagely. "Me, I nevair make mistake."

Alex, unseen, pulled a face into the telephone receiver. Danielle prattled on, regardless.

"*Bien sûr*, it is not everyone zat is noticing zese sings. I sink 'e doesn' make it too obvious, no? When I am talking wiz ze leetle one I see zat she is not knowing, and so I say to myself, you will not let ze cat out of ze basket, Danielle . . . *occupe-toi de tes oignons!* And so I am silent like ze tomb. *Quand même*, it cannot be too long, I sink, before *la petite* is—'ow do you say? When ze eye is made to be open? *Désabusée*—and when zat is 'appening—"

The cab, heaven be praised, turned up within minutes. He bundled Danielle off as tactfully as he could and was on his way back down the passage when the telephone rang. He almost ignored it, but habit was too strong. He snatched up the receiver and said "Yes! Hello!" in militant tones intended to convey to whoever it was that he had neither the time nor the inclination for an idle gossiping session.

"Alex?" It was Nicky. He sounded somewhat distraught. "Have you got Gill there?"

"Yes, I have! What the hell has been going on?"

"I'll tell you later. I'm coming straight round."

"*Nicky!*" He bellowed it down the receiver, but too late: the boy had already hung up. He turned back, with foreboding, to the kitchen. Gill had made two cups of coffee and was perched on the edge of the table eating some stale digestive biscuits that he had put to one side for the birds. She was not crying any more. Her eyes were quite dry, no trace of a tear. Hard to believe that only ten minutes ago she had been weeping in his arms.

"Was that Nicky?" she said.

"Yes. He's on his way round. He—"

"I don't want to see him."

"What?"

"*I don't want to see him!*" She crumpled the digestive biscuit packet into a ball. "You can just tell him to go away again. Your coffee's getting cold."

He ignored the coffee.

"Why don't you want to see him?"

"Because I don't. *He* knows. Ask him."

"Gilly, *I'm* asking you. I—" Just in time, he managed to restrain himself. *Gently*, he had said to Nicky. *Gently . . .* "All right, sweetheart. All right. If you don't want to tell me, you don't have to. It's none of my business anyway."

There was a silence. Alex shrugged his shoulders. Gill, with slow deliberation, slipped off the table, went across to the sink. She lifted the lid of the waste bin, dropped in the crumpled biscuit packet.

"Actually, if you must know—" she turned, defiantly, to face him—"I just happened to go walking in at the wrong moment, that's all."

Alex closed his eyes.

"Oh, my God!" Could that wretched boy *never* do anything right? Must he constantly be making a hash of things? *Gently*, he had said. *Break it gently*—

"He had his little friend in there. His name's Gino. He puts cocktail sticks into cherries. He looks a bit daft, but apparently he can't help it, he's deaf and dumb. It seems an odd choice, doesn't it? When you've got the whole world at your feet . . . Still—" she snatched up her empty coffee cup and began vigorously swilling it out beneath the cold water tap—"I daresay they're happy together. They certainly looked it."

"Gilly—" Alex took a step forward. He stopped. "For God's *sake!*" he said. "What is the matter with that boy?"

Gill gave a little laugh; light and scornful.

"I should have thought that was perfectly obvious," she said.

There was a distinctly waspish tinge to her voice. It wasn't like Gill. She was not the girl for being bitchy, no matter how upset she was. Tears he could understand, he could deal with; but that she should actually turn against Nicky—that was totally unexpected. It threw him, for a moment, off balance.

"Drink your coffee," she said.

Mechanically, he took up his cup. The coffee was cold and rather bitter. *I just happened to go walking in at the wrong moment . . .* Why, oh why, could he not just have done as Nicky had wanted him to do and break it to her himself? That way they would all have been spared a lot of embarrassment. Now, for the life of him, he could think of nothing adequate to say. There really wasn't very much that could be said, other than perhaps by Nicky himself. He disposed of his cold coffee in three quick gulps, took his empty cup across to her at the sink.

"Gilly, I know it's a hell of a thing to have happened, and I'm certainly not making any excuses for him, but—"

"But if I'd had my wits about me I'd have guessed long ago." She snatched the cup from him. "I'm so innocent, aren't I?

Twenty years old and I'm still so *innocent* . . . I'm still so *naïve* . . . It's about time I grew up and started to learn about these things. For goodness sake, anyone would think I'd been brought up in a *nunnery*. A child of two could have seen it, it's so obvious."

"Now you're being unfair—both to yourself and to him. It's not in the least obvious. You—"

"Oh, you don't have to *defend* him," she said. "I'm not attacking him. I daresay he can't *help* it. Anyway, he didn't know I was going to come barging in. I told him I was going to be away for the whole of the weekend—he probably thought he was quite safe. Now, I suppose, he'll think I was spying on him. Not that I was—not that it matters any more. It's all—" She broke off, at the sound of the front door being opened. "That's Nicky. I don't want to see him."

"Gill—sweetheart—I really think you—"

"No!" She banged the cup down on to the draining board and turned, dark eyes burning. "Send him away! I don't want to see him!"

She remained adamant. He spent the next thirty minutes shuttling back and forth between a distraught Nicky in the sitting-room and Gill, stiff and unyielding, in the kitchen. Not all his pleas on Nicky's behalf would move her; she only pursed her lips and reiterated that she didn't want to see him. From feeling the strongest urge to wring the boy's neck, he began in the end, in spite of himself, to have some faint stirrings of sympathy for him. He was too obviously and too genuinely distressed at what had occurred for wrath to endure very long.

"I wouldn't have had it happen for the world, I swear to you, I'd no idea she was going to come walking in like that. If I had, I would never—believe me, Alex, I would *never*—I mean, for God's sake! All these months . . . can't you make her see me? *Please?* Just for one minute? Just so that I can tell her?"

He wasn't quite sure what telling her was likely to achieve, but obediently he went back and tried one more time to persuade her—and one more time without success.

"I don't want to see him," she said.

"But sweetheart, tomorrow morning you're going to have to see him whether you like it or not."

"Tomorrow morning is tomorrow morning. I don't want to see him *now*."

"You mean I've really got to send him away? Like this?" She looked at him, contemptuously.

"Like what?"

"Without being able to talk to you—without being able to tell you how sorry he is."

"Sorry!"

"He's very unhappy, Gilly. You might at least give him a chance to explain."

Her lip curled.

"What is there to explain?"

What, indeed? She had surely already received all the explanation that was necessary? He said, rather lamely:

"Well . . . why it happened, why he—"

"I know why it happened! It happened because for once *I* wasn't there, hanging around, getting in the way . . . for once he could have the place to himself and stop pretending. So from now on he can always have it to himself. He can do just whatever he likes. He doesn't have to pretend any more. *I* don't care . . . why don't you tell him to hurry back before this little friend gets tired of waiting and goes off to find someone else?"

He didn't deliver the suggestion in quite that form, but Nicky was capable of reading between the lines.

"Does she hate me?" he said.

"Of course she doesn't hate you."

"But she still won't talk to me?"

"Look, Nicky—" he placed his hands on the boy's shoulders. "Just try to see it from her point of view . . . that kid has worshipped you for as far back as I can remember. I don't doubt she's had all sorts of dreams about you—and now, quite suddenly, you've gone and shoved a battering ram through the whole lot. Yes, all right, I know, you never meant it to happen, it was just unfortunate, it couldn't be helped; I'm not blaming you —not at any rate for this. I still hold you responsible for letting her move in with you, but we've already had that one out. In this instance, I agree, it was just one of those things. But the fact is, whether you like it or not, it's happened. You can't expect her to come to terms with it all at once, she needs time to get used to the idea."

"You didn't seem to," said Nicky.

"No. Well—I haven't spent the better part of my life being in love with you, have I? It didn't exactly shatter any of my romantic illusions . . . Now, go on, push off back to whatever-his-name-is and leave Gill to me. You're only making matters worse jittering about here."

"Well, tell her, if she changes her mind—"

"I'll tell her," said Alex. "I'll tell her."

"And tell her, for God's sake, that it doesn't mean I don't *love* her!"

He did tell her, but it made no visible impression. She sat in stony silence as he did his best to salvage for her what was yet left to be salvaged from the crumbling ruins of her illusions. He thought at one point she wasn't even listening, but then, quite suddenly, the tears welled up in her eyes and she said:

"He should have told me . . . he should have *told* me!"

"You mean—" he hesitated. "About the boy?"

"No! Everything! Not just *him* . . . everything!"

"Oh, Gilly." He took her hands in his. "Don't be too hard on him. He never meant you to find out this way."

"Then why didn't he *tell* me? *Years* ago?"

"Maybe he didn't realize . . . years ago. Even if he did—it's not a very easy thing to tell, is it? Especially not when it's somebody you care about."

"So why didn't *you* tell me? Letting me go on like that . . . making a fool of myself—all this time—" She tipped her head back, defying the tears to spill over. "Everybody knowing except *me!*"

"Sweetheart, that's not true . . . everybody doesn't know except you. How could everybody know and you not get to hear of it? In *that* hive of gossip?"

"Well, but *you* must have known!"

"I didn't, Gilly. I promise you." Not, in truth, that the news had come as any great surprise to him, not that from time to time he had not speculated, but with so little to go on, and then with Gill moving into the flat—the wonder of it was, the boy should have been so extraordinarily discreet for as long as he had. *I sink 'e doesn' make it too obvious, no?* For one so naturally flamboyant as Nicky, it must have been a labour of Hercules. He said as much to Gill, hoping to raise a smile, however reluctant, but she only turned her head away and said:

"*She* knew."

"She?"

"Danielle . . . I heard her—I couldn't help hearing her. She's got a voice like a corncrake. Of course, she would know, wouldn't she? *She* never makes mistakes."

So that was it. Not only the shattering of romantic daydreams, but a touch of hurt pride into the bargain. Well, it was not to be wondered at. Doubtless she had already built up in her injured mind a picture of the sniggering hordes. He shook his head.

"Don't confuse Danielle with the rest of the Company. She's hardly representative. They haven't all got her special antennae. And let's face it, sweetheart—be realistic." He winked at her. "It's not really earth-shaking, is it? Mm? Not in this business . . . who do you think's likely to bat an eyelid? Would *you* bat an eyelid? If it were anyone but Nicky? Of course you wouldn't. You're far too blasé. It's old hat, you've seen it all. So try and cheer up, there's a good girl, because it's not the end of the world. After all, what difference is it going to make? Nicky's still Nicky, isn't he? He's just the same as he always was."

But he wasn't, of course; not to Gill. How could he be?

7

SHE didn't go back again to Guilford Street. Alex called round there next day in the car to collect her things, but didn't press her to accompany him. As a result he neglected to bring her mascot, her lucky pixie, which Nicky had found for her years ago on the beach at Brighton. It was only an ordinary, common-or-garden, present-from-Cornwall sort of pixie, but it was the first gift she had ever received from him and in all these years she had never been without it. She told herself now that she didn't care. The pixie could stay where it was, out of sight and forgotten at the back of her handkerchief drawer: she had no more use for it. Unfortunately, the habit was too deeply ingrained to be thus easily jettisoned. Bad luck began to dog her—she tripped on the stone steps leading to her dressing-room and grazed her elbow, stubbed her toe quite badly against a kerbstone, was viciously scratched in the face by Nanty's cat. She put it all down to the loss of her lucky pixie. She might have asked Nicky to bring it in for her, but that was out of the question. She was not having *him* suspect it was still of any importance.

On Friday afternoon, when she knew him to be safely out of the way at a photo session, she called round herself to the flat and found the boy, Gino, there. He was seated at the table, pencil in hand, head bent over a sheet of paper, and looked up with a start as the door opened. Plainly, he was every bit as disconcerted by the encounter as she. He pushed back his chair and rose awkwardly to his feet, putting his pencil to his mouth and chewing at the end of it like a child caught doing something that it knows it has no right to do. Gill said stiffly:

"I've come to collect something."

Whether he understood her or not she had no idea, but he took the pencil out of his mouth and nodded at her and smiled, in a manner quite obviously intended to convey goodwill; then rapidly, in a series of gestures too clear to be mistaken, proceeded to offer her a cup of something. *Him* to be offering *her* a cup—*him*, in this very flat where only a few days ago she had been living in blissful ignorance of the fact that he even existed. He didn't give her a chance to say no: he was already halfway across the room towards the kitchen. She shrugged her shoulders. Let him waste his time making tea or coffee, if that was what he wanted. She had no intention of staying to drink it.

As she passed the table she glanced down at the work on which he had been so industriously engaged and saw that it was a half-finished portrait of Nicky, a more polished version of the one she had found in his bedroom the other day. Then she had thought it rather good; now she dismissed it as the mere scrawling of an untrained amateur. She fetched her lucky pixie from its hiding place at the back of her dressing table drawer and was relieved to note that the room was just as she had left it. She had half feared that it might already have been taken over—not that the absence of alien possessions was necessarily anything to go by. He obviously had the free run of the flat. Just because he didn't appear to be actually *sleeping* in her room—She resisted the temptation to go and look in Nicky's. She reminded herself that she didn't care any more: that from now on Nicky could do just whatever he liked.

Knowing full well that she was being cowlike, she nevertheless walked out of the flat without even taking the trouble to put her head round the kitchen door and announce the fact—which was not only rude and unpleasant, but pettily spiteful into the bargain. He would come out of the kitchen, with his two cups of whatever it was he was making, and not having heard the front door would expect her still to be there. He would go looking for her all over the flat, from one room to another, wondering where she could have got to. It was a mean trick to have played;

so mean that she very nearly turned and went back again, but then half way down the stairs she met Manuela on her way up.

Manuela was bearing before her one of her famous dishes of Spanish slops—Nicky always referred to it as Spanish slops. No one but Manuela knew exactly what it was or what went into it, but it was one of her greatest delicacies and reserved only for special favourites. Gill had never been a favourite of any kind. She had often suspected, indeed, that Manuela had looked upon her as a usurper and as a rival, and had resented her being there in the flat at all. Her successor, evidently, had already managed to ingratiate himself: mere passing reference to the fact that he was up there was sufficient to produce a maternal beam and a sentimental "*Ah, sí! El pobre!*" Gill wondered whether she would still beam and call him *el pobre* were she to be told the exact nature of his relationship with Nicky. The chances were that she probably would. The field had at any rate been cleared of all *female* competition; that in itself was enough for Manuela.

Had her dreams only been other than they were, it might perhaps have been enough for Gill. She had lain awake at night—that very first night—trying to convince herself, trying without success to philosophize. Better a Gino than a Danielle—better a Gino than a Gundi. At least Nicky had not neglected her in favour of another girl; that surely must be of *some* comfort? In theory it might have been: in practice it failed her miserably. Nicky had come up to her in class, first thing Monday morning.

"Gilly, please!" he had said.

He had stretched out both hands: she had ignored them. She had been very conscious of the fact that Danielle was only a few paces away, an interested spectator of the scene. For the sake of appearance it would have been wiser, without any doubt, to have forced herself to behave normally, as if no rift had ever opened up between the two of them, but that, at the time, had not occurred to her. All that had occurred to her at the time was her own wounded pride and the need to do something hurtful in return. Coldly, she had turned her back on him.

"I don't want to talk about it."

Several times over the next few days he had approached her, doing his best to make the peace. At last, in despair, he had said:

"We've still got to dance together, you know—or would you rather put in for a change of partner?"

"Is that what you want?" she said.

"It's not what *I* want! I'm not the one who's keeping up the quarrel."

"There hasn't been any quarrel."

"Then why won't you talk to me?"

"I will talk to you. I just don't want to discuss—a certain subject, that's all."

It wasn't all, of course; they both knew that. They went on dancing together, but it wasn't the same as it had been. However much they might strive, like the good professionals they were, not to let personal relationships interfere with work, the atmosphere between them continued strained. How could it be otherwise? When he was thinking, all the time, of *him*—when all this while they had been bound up with each other, and she nothing but an incumbrance, her very presence an embarrassment because it kept them apart—how could the atmosphere, now, be anything *but* strained?

Madame, who was never one to approve of personal relationships within the ranks of the Company in any case, watched them closely but said nothing; then suddenly, without warning, announced the postponement of *Adam* until the following spring. No explanation was given. It was left to Alex, admittedly more in her confidence than most, to interpret the decision. It had, according to him, been based solely on expediency. Christmas had not seemed such a good time of year, after all, to be introducing a new and controversial work into the repertoire. At the end of January they were off on another provincial tour—to try it out then would plainly be asking for trouble. Far better wait until the new season. Gill was by no means certain that she believed him, but at all events, whatever the true reason behind the postponement, it was a weight off her mind. Playing Temptress to Nicky was the last thing she felt herself fit for just at this moment. (If she could not do it before, how could she hope to do it *now*, knowing, as she did, that she stood no chance at all?)

It was, of course, inevitable that the rest of the Company should quickly sense that all was not well between the two of them. Even apart from the fact that she now came in by car with Alex every morning, her own attitude towards Nicky must sooner or later have alerted them. Nicky himself did his best, never a day passed but he would hold out some fresh olive branch, demonstrating to her in a thousand different ways that he was still as anxious as ever for a reconciliation. He gave her all the openings she could possibly have asked for: she ignored them each and every one. She knew that she was being unreasonable, for no matter what he had done he deserved a fair hearing, but still that wounded pride inside her was smarting, still crying out for its revenge. More than once she had been on the point of throwing her arms about him and telling him how much she loved him in spite of everything; more than once she had opened her mouth to beg his forgiveness for the way she had been treating him. Always, at the last moment, visions of the boy, Gino, had risen up and choked the words in her throat. Why should *she* be the one to apologize? She had done nothing wrong, she had committed no crime. She was only reacting, and quite justifiably, to a situation which he himself had created.

He bore with it for a fortnight, patiently enduring all that she threw at him, all her snubs, all her sneers, all her pieces of gratuitous nastiness; until, one morning, in front of other people, she went too far even for Nicky. There had been just a handful of them there, waiting in the rehearsal room until Madame should arrive to conduct a run-through of her own *Gala Creation*, being temporarily brought back into the repertoire in place of *Adam*. It required only the four couples, Alex and Andrea, herself and Nicky, István, Zoë, Derek, Tanya. Derek had not yet put in an appearance, but the rest of them were all there, István and Zoë studiously at work on their variation, marking it out in the corner, Andrea sitting on a chair, placidly knitting at something long and limp and shapeless, Nicky fooling about, pseudo-amorous, with Tanya, Gill herself leaning against the barre with Alex, pretending not to notice. Much she cared if he chose to conduct meaningless flirtations in front of her. Let him get on with it. He was only doing it to pay her out. He had come up to her earlier on and put his arms round her and said "Give us a cuddle?" It had been one of those moments when she had been sorely tempted, but then again the vision of that smooth, olive-skinned face with its big brown eyes had risen before her, and she had pushed him away with a disdainful "Hadn't you better keep that sort of thing for your boyfriend?" He hadn't come near her again. She could hardly blame him now for a bit of ostentatious byplay, but he needn't think it riled her, because it didn't. His antics left her completely cold. Not so Derek. He, walking in in the middle of the performance, took one look and in tones of disgust said: "God in heaven! Can't that fellow *ever* keep his hands off other people's property? What's the matter with him? You keep him on short rations, or something?"

It proved the last straw. Before she could stop herself, she heard her own voice, clear and carrying:

"You shouldn't let it worry you so much. It's not as if he's likely to *do* anything to her."

All over the rehearsal room, a silence fell. No one actually ceased activities—István and Zoë went on with their marking, Andrea with her knitting, not even Nicky or Tanya gave any signs of having heard the remark; it was obvious, all the same, that they had. Everybody must have done so—doubtless it was no more than she had intended. Derek, the only one not able to seek refuge in pretence, since the words had been specifically directed at him, was quite plainly embarrassed. He grinned, rather feebly, and said: "Well, heaven help him if he does, that's all I can say," and he chuckled as he said it, just to show that of course it was all a joke. Somehow, it did not carry quite as much conviction as it might have done. The relief when the door opened to admit Madame, in all her usual regality, was almost audible.

The rehearsal which followed was quite dreadful. All the old rapport which had existed between Nicky and herself had been destroyed at a blow by her own malicious tongue. Nicky said not a word more to her than was strictly necessary, either then or for the rest of the day— indeed, she hardly even saw him for the rest of the day save when they were on stage together. Whether he was purposely avoiding her she could not have said, for she was herself too busy avoiding him. If she could only have taken back those words that she had spoken, how gladly would she have done so. She had hated herself for them before they were even half way out of her mouth. She felt guilty enough without Alex, on the drive back to Clapham that same night, seeing fit to rebuke her. She needed no rebuke to tell her that she had behaved shabbily. What she had said was inexcusable; she knew it well enough—and yet some demon even now made her toss her head and stubbornly declare herself unrepentant.

"What does it matter if people know the truth at last? He ought to thank me for it—at least he won't have to go on pretending any more. In any case, he doesn't care two straws what anyone thinks."

It was what he had told her, wasn't it? That night he had stayed at home and made love to her (and how he must have enjoyed *that*) and then refused to take her over to the Hereford lest someone mistake her for his little brother? *It doesn't bother* me one way or the other. They can think what they like as far as I'm concerned . . .

"If he really didn't care," said Alex, "why do you imagine he's been at such pains all these years to be discreet about it?"

"I don't know." If he hadn't meant it, he shouldn't have said it. He always had been vainglorious. "Probably didn't want you finding out."

"Why me?"

"Well, you're about the only person whose good opinion he's ever really valued, so—"

"So he knows perfectly well he's not likely to have forfeited it just for a thing like this. Hell's bells! I'm no moralist to be sitting in judgement on other people's fads and fancies. Live and let live's good enough for me."

Gill felt the colour rise in her cheeks. Was he implying that she was a moralist? That she sat in judgement? It wasn't true. She cared not one jot how other people chose to conduct their private lives—

other people. That was it, wasn't it? *Other* people; not Nicky.

"Sweetheart, believe me," said Alex, "I do realize that it's not easy for you. I do appreciate that. But don't you think you could try to be just the tiniest little bit more understanding? The last thing he ever meant to do was hurt you."

She looked frostily ahead of her through the windscreen.

"He hasn't hurt me."

"You mean you're just angry with him?"

She hunched a shoulder. Alex took a quick glance down at her as he brought the car to a halt at a set of traffic lights.

"You know, I blame that boy for a whole lot of things," he said, "but in all honesty I can't entirely blame him for this. I'm not making any excuses for him, I told you that before; but if this is the way things are, then this is the way things are, and there really isn't an awful lot that he can be expected to do about it. I think sooner or later that's something you're going to have to accept. You can't hold it against him for all time."

She didn't hold it against him—she wasn't even angry with him; not in her heart of hearts. There was just a hard knot of bitterness inside her which refused to be untied.

Nicky hadn't bothered any more, after that, about being discreet. He had obviously seen no further reason for it. If that was the way things were, then that was the way things were; why should it trouble him who knew? On Saturday evening Derek and Tanya had thrown an impromptu party—"everyone round our place after the show". Alex hadn't gone because he wasn't a very partified sort of person, Gill hadn't gone because she wasn't in a very partified sort of mood, but first thing Monday morning quite half a dozen members of the Company had kindly taken the trouble to inform her that Nicky had turned up and that he had brought "a friend" along with him. They made it very obvious that when they said "friend", in inverted commas, they really meant something else. She knew full well that they were watching her, eager to see how she would react: she refused to be drawn. She said simply, "Oh, really? Which one was that?" in tones the most casual that she could muster. What was it to her that Nicky should go taking strange boys along to parties with him? Let him, if that was what amused him. Let him make a spectacle of himself. It was no concern of hers. She was only glad that she had not chosen to be present. Mercifully, they spared her the details, but from the none too veiled hints she was left in not very much doubt that he had finally thrown caution to the winds. She asked Kath, who had gone along with her stockbroker, but Kath was evasive and said only:

"Well—you know—"

"No, I do not know!" she said. "Tell me!"

"Well—" Kath plainly would have preferred not to. "He just—"

"Just what? Sat on the sofa and held hands all evening?"

From the look on Kath's face, she knew she was not so very far from the truth. The news, of course, spread as quickly as news of that sort always did. Before the week was half over, it was common property that *Nicky—can you believe?—was knocking himself out over some pretty little Eyetie . . .*

Had he only been content with dragging the boy along to parties she could have maintained a fair show of indifference, for parties, after all, could be stayed away from, she was under no compulsion to go along and be provoked, but then he started bringing him into the theatre as well, flaunting him under her nose in an open gesture of defiance, and any show of indifference, after that, became well nigh impossible. How could she pretend not to care? Every time she saw them together it was like a knife to the heart. He was doing it on purpose, of course; she realized that. By seeking to humiliate him in front of his colleagues, she had pushed him just that little bit too far. Now he, in return, was humiliating her before the entire Company. It was as if he were saying, "All right, you've asked for it . . . now see how you like it."

By some alchemy he even managed to persuade Madame into granting one of her rare dispensations for the boy to attend rehearsals, to come backstage during performances, so that soon there was almost no way of escaping from him, wherever you turned you found him there with his pencil and his sketch pad, cluttering up the wings, getting under people's feet. It might have been easier to bear if the rest of the Company had shared her irritation, but far from it, they actually went out of their way to encourage him, clamouring like cretins for instant portraits. It seemed the boy was no amateur, after all. It was he who had been responsible for the ceramics she had seen at the *Drei Sterne*—there was even talk of his being commissioned to design the costumes for *Adam*.

"Ridiculous!" said Gill. "What does he know about it?"

"He is quite good," said Kath. "Honestly, Gilly. He did a super picture of Nicky—"

"I saw it," she said. "I thought it was rather primitive. Really! All this fuss. Just because a boy who's deaf and dumb has learnt how to pick up a pencil and make a few daubs on a sheet of paper . . . what's so remarkable about that?"

She was cutting off her nose to spite her face. It would have been both more generous and more honest to admit that the boy had talent. His pencil was his main means of communication; to deny him that was to deny him everything— was simply to parade her own wounded pride in public. He had, in any case, all the cards stacked on his side. Even she could not deny him his good looks, but more than that there was a quality of waiflike innocence about him, a winsome appeal that everyone except, apparently, herself, found quite impossible to resist. Personally it struck her as rather nauseating. If—which she very much doubted —he had been innocent before, he certainly wasn't innocent now, so why pretend? He knew what he was about, all right: he knew which side his bread was buttered. He was just taking Nicky for a ride. All that big-eyed wonderment, all that seeming devotion, that following about like a shadow—he would be off like a flash the minute he found something better. She really wondered that Nicky should allow himself to be so hood-winked.

Unfortunately, if Nicky were hood-winked, so were all the rest of the Company. Within only a matter of weeks, the boy had become a firm favourite. Even Madame had been observed once or twice to call a temporary halt on her ceremonial progress about the theatre in order to adjust her reading spectacles and gaze her august approval upon the ubiqui-tous sketch pad. Even Alex—and that, surely, must rank as the final treachery? —even he, one morning, with unthinking affection, had ruffled his hair as he

walked past him. Gill alone, of all the
Company, held herself aloof. Whenever
their paths crossed—which they did all
too frequently for her liking—the boy
always nodded at her and smiled, obviously eager to establish friendly relations,
but she would have none of it. He might
pull the wool over everyone else's eyes:
he wasn't pulling it over hers. It was as
much as she could do even to acknowl-
edge his presence. That she was only
making matters worse for herself, she was
very well aware. As Alex had said, she
would have to come to terms with the
situation sooner or later, she could not for
ever go on bearing grudges. Had she only
forced herself right at the very beginning
to at least a pretence of acceptance, the
dressing gossip that simmered and
bubbled even now would have died down
weeks ago. It would have been a nine
days' wonder. There would have been a
few *fancy that's* and *well I never's*, the
usual chorus of *I always knew, you can
always tell, I'm not in the least surprised*,
from the wise-after-the-eventers, and then

some fresh subject would have claimed their attention and that would be that, past history. It was Gill herself, with her intransigent hostility, who was supplying all the fuel that kept the fires alight. She had no need to put her ear to any keyholes to hear the busy buzz of wagging tongues. She could guess well enough the general run of speculation: had she and Nicky ever *really*—or had they always been just—but then if *that* were the case—

Kath, ever faithful, striving valiantly to remain loyal to Gill even as she openly fraternized with the enemy, sought to comfort her by saying that "it probably won't last more than five minutes, you know these things never do". It was what she herself had said to Kath about Alex and Danielle. It hadn't been of much solace to Kath, then; it wasn't of much solace to Gill now. What if it didn't last five minutes? He still would not want her —not in the way that she wanted him. *Had* wanted him. She said gloomily: "At least you had your stockbroker to fall back on."

"Well, but you've got Alex," pointed out Kath.

"Not in that way, I haven't."

"I'm sure you could have, if you played your cards right."

She was too eaten up, at the time, with self-pity, to attach any significance to the words.

"From now on," she said, "I'm giving up playing cards. I quite obviously don't have any card sense . . . I'd make a terrible poker player."

Alex in his turn, with unconscious irony, sought to pour balm on her wounds by assuring her on the contrary that it was *not* "just a five-minute job".

"He'd never have run the risk of upsetting you for some cheap backstreet *affaire*. Grant him that much. He does seem to have some genuine feeling for the boy. At least it's bucked his ideas up a bit, I'll say that for him—actually considering someone else beside number one for a change. I never thought the day would come when I'd see *him* taking responsibility for another human being."

If he were under the impression that he was bringing her any comfort, then he could not have been more mistaken. It brought her no comfort at all—more like the exact opposite. A cheap backstreet *affaire* she could have stood without too much heartache, but was this not the very thing she had always most dreaded, that someone, some day, should succeed in engaging his affections? It was that which twisted the knife in the wound—Nicky taking responsibility for another human being, Nicky thinking of someone else beside himself. He had never taken responsibility for her. He had never caught *her* eye across a roomful of people and winked at her, and smiled, as if to enclose just the two of them in a private world of their own. *She* had never had any sense of being his, to be guarded and protected. Never in any way had he been proprietory towards her. It was the very fact, now, that he *was* emotionally involved, and plainly cared not who knew it, that caused all the pain. Alex had said that Nicky never meant to hurt her; but every time she saw him with his arm about the boy's shoulders it cut her to the very quick.

Vic rang one Sunday morning from the *Drei Sterne*, wanting to speak to her. She told Alex to say that she was out. Whatever Vic had to say to her, she didn't want to hear it. She hated everyone, at that moment, who had anything to do with the *Drei Sterne. They* must have known what was going on. Vic, indeed, could have told her years ago, if only he would, that she was simply wasting her time as far as Nicky was concerned. Instead he had let her continue, making a fool of herself. As for that Gundi, acting as go-between—making telephone calls, arranging assignations—she must have thought she was as green as grass—and had she not been so? When she thought back to that night when Nicky had made love to her—when she realized that what he had done afterwards was to go and ring Trudi in order to let *him* know that he wouldn't be able to get over that evening—he must have resented every minute of the time that he had spent with her. And then staying indoors all the nights that followed, pacing the flat like a caged tiger, reflecting, no doubt, that if it hadn't been for *her*—and then the girl, Gundi, telephoning him, and him taking off like greased lightning, *I'm sorry, Gilly, I'm afraid I'm going to have to go out after all* . . . What had she said to him, that evening on the telephone? *He* wants you, so drop everything and come? Or words to that effect. And so, of course, he had obediently dropped everything and gone, and certainly it wasn't his fault, certainly he had never encouraged her in any way whatsoever, she had nothing with which to reproach him except that he ought to have told her. If he had only taken her into his confidence, instead of always so rigorously excluding her, she might now have been able to share in the fact that he was happy, instead of hating and resenting him for it. If he had only been prepared to trust her, to allow her some share, be it never so small, in that jealously guarded private life of his—she would have realized, early on, that there was no point in daydreaming. She would have loved him just as dearly, but she would have loved him differently. That was all.

Christmas came and was more of a nightmare than a festival. It was quite the worst Christmas they had had since the year that Gill's mother had died. The actual day itself they had always, the three of them, spent together. Even Nicky had regarded it as something sacred. He had been used to joke that he "only came home to please Alexis", but when once, thoughtlessly, as a teenager, she had suggested that he and she should do something different, should go away somewhere by themselves, he had been quite shocked and had read her a long lecture about how this was the one time of year when they most certainly should *not* go off and do something by themselves. This Christmas was the first over which there had hung any real question mark. When Alex said "Well? And what are we going to do?" he had made it very plain that the decision was with her. Nicky would not come by himself, they both of them knew that. She had either to accept Nicky plus Gino or for the first time ever they would spend their Christmas apart—and the separation would be as much mental as physical. She said grudgingly: "I suppose we shall have to put up with him."

"If you mean Gino," said Alex, "then only if you're prepared to treat him properly."

She tossed her head. *Her* treat *him* properly!

"How is one supposed to treat him?"

"Preferably as if he's a human being. You can't invite the boy round here and then behave as if he's suffering from leprosy—not unless you want Nicky getting uptight and walking out, for which I can't honestly say I should blame him."

"Hm!"

"I mean it, Gilly . . . seriously. Unless you're going to be nice to him—"

"Oh, I'll be *nice* to him, if that's what you want."

"It is what I want. I'm very well aware of the way you feel—everyone's aware of the way you feel—but I'm not having Nicky upset over Christmas" (Nicky! What about her?) "and as a matter of fact if you'd just make the initial effort you'd find it wasn't anywhere near as difficult as you thought. It doesn't take much, for heaven's sake—you've only got to smile at him once or twice and show willing. He's really not such a bad little kid."

"No, I'm sure," she said. "Everyone loves him but me."

"Well, Nicky certainly seems to, which is the only thing that matters. I'm afraid, sweetheart, whether you like it or not, that that is something you're going to have to reconcile yourself to."

She tried very hard, and so, too, did Nicky. Either from natural tact, or more likely because Alex had warned him against doing anything to provoke, he was obviously, and rather painfully, on his best behaviour. He sat on one side of the room, the boy sat on the other, ostentatiously they avoided all contact. That still didn't stop them being very much aware of each other. Gill, obedient to her promise, forced herself to smile and did her best not to notice. It wasn't very easy —perhaps it wasn't very easy for them, either. She wondered what Alex had said. *Look, just cool it, OK? She's prepared to accept it, but you don't have to go shoving it in her face . . .* Something like that. She could hear him saying it. Towards midday they went out to the kitchen to check how dinner was progressing. Nicky said: "Do you want us to come and do things? Peel spuds or something?" Normally when he said "us" he meant the three of them—cooking the Christmas dinner had always been a communal effort; now he meant just the two. It was Alex who said "No, that's all right. You stay here. We'll see to it." He, of course, meant herself and him. Going back unexpectedly into the sitting-room she had found the two of them together. They had sprung apart, guiltily, like a couple of scalded cats. She had known then, for sure, that Alex must have said something. She could almost have wished that he hadn't. Nicky, ever intolerant of any form of restriction, spent the rest of the day like a tethered animal, growing hourly and more obviously frustrated. She felt that were he not bound, like herself, to a promise extracted under duress, he would have snatched the boy into his arms there and then with a defiant "The hell with it! This is the way it is, you can like it or lump it."

She wouldn't have liked it, certainly; but she was inclined to think that anything would be better than this most unnatural restraint. The boy himself was plainly ill at ease, shy of doing anything to upset *her*, she was tense and withdrawn, Alex was having to try just that little bit too hard to ring totally true. Even Nanty seemed to catch the prevailing atmosphere, refusing point-blank to be coaxed into coming down to join them but roundly declaring she would "stay up here where I know that I'm wanted". No amount of cajolery on Nicky's part could prevail upon her to change her mind, and when, in the end, they took her dinner up to her on a tray, she simply put it on the floor for the cat.

"I'm afraid the poor old love is finally going off her chump," said Nicky.

Gill, without thinking, said: "She always gets worked up when there are strangers in the house."

It was a simple statement of fact: it hadn't been meant as a dig. Nicky, nevertheless, was instantly on the defensive.

"Look, if you didn't want us to come—"

"I didn't say I didn't want you to come! I just said that she gets worked up, that's all."

"So that's my fault?"

"I didn't *say* it was your fault. I—"

"Children, children, do we have to?" Alex had put an arm round each and reproachfully shaken his head. "If you must quarrel, at least quarrel about something worth while." They had not quarrelled, but still, between them, for some time afterwards, there had simmered an unvoiced antagonism. At one point in the evening, briefly, they had found themselves alone together. There had been a slight, awkward pause, then Nicky, as if suddenly making up his mind to one last effort at appeasement, had stepped across to her as she knelt by the fire, and holding out both hands had said: "Come on, Gilly . . . give us a kiss and let's be friends again. I'm not untouchable, am I? Look—" he had taken down a sprig of mistletoe from above the mantelshelf—"Christmas kiss like old times . . . how about it?"

She had nearly—oh, so very nearly!—scrambled to her feet and thrown her arms about his neck and hugged him just as hard as she could; but then the door had opened and *he* had come in, and spite like a poisoned dart had pierced her tongue.

"I should have thought he's the one you ought to be asking, not me!"

How could she blame him if he took her at her word? For one long moment he had stood there, looking down at her, the sprig of mistletoe still clasped in his hand; then slowly and deliberately, he had tossed the mistletoe on to the fire.

"Come on." He had put an arm about the boy's shoulders. "Let's go home."

It was Alex who came to her and took her in his arms as she sat sobbing by the fire.

"Alex, I tried," she said, "I did try!"

"I know you did, darling." He held her head into his shoulder, gently stroking her hair. "Perhaps I shouldn't have asked it of you . . . it's just that you and Nicky mean all the world to me, and it breaks my heart to see you tearing each other to pieces."

8

HAD she only known how brief a spell of happiness Nicky was to be allowed, she surely would not have grudged it him? Scarcely two weeks later and it had all come to an end. It was a distraught Tanya who had broken it to them.

"Where's Alex?" She had seized upon Gill as she came into the theatre for the evening performance. "*Where's Alex?*"

"He's right behind me. Why? What's—"

"Alex!" She had rushed at him. "Thank heavens you're here! I've been praying you'd turn up early, I tried ringing you only there wasn't any reply and—"

"Hey, now! Just take it easy. Calm down . . . what's all the panic?"

"It's Nicky—oh, Alex, I think you

ought to go to him! Something's—something's happened. To Gino—"

"To *Gino?*"

"Yes, he's—the police—they came round here—I—"

"All right, all right." Alex took her by the shoulders. "Now tell me . . . what's happened?"

What had happened had been all too tragically simple. Nicky that afternoon had had a matinée, *Carnaval* and *Tricorne*. Gill and Alex had been in the former, not in the latter. They had left the theatre and gone back home for the rest of the afternoon. Nicky had come off stage at the end of the second ballet to find the police there waiting to speak to him.

"They said there'd—there'd been an accident. Gino was in hospital—"

He had, apparently, set out from Guilford Street to meet Nicky as arranged at the theatre. There had been a thick fog at the time, visibility down almost to nil: he, being unable to hear any approaching traffic, had stepped off the kerb straight into the path of an oncoming vehicle. Tanya had gone with Nicky to the hospital, but they had been too late. He had already been dead when they got there.

"Oh, my God—"

Alex wiped a hand across his brow. His face, beneath its freckles, had turned quite ashen. Neither he nor Tanya took the slightest bit of notice of Gill. She might almost not have existed.

"I didn't know what to do," said Tanya. "I wanted to call a cab and come straight round to you, but he wouldn't, he—"

"Where is he now?"

"He's back here—in his dressing room. He—"

"How's he taking it?"

"I—" She shook her head. "I don't know. He says he's all right—he says he's going on. Derek's in there with him. He tried to give him some brandy, but he won't touch it. I'm sure he ought to have something, he—"

"OK, I'll go to him." Alex squeezed her hand. "Thanks, Tanya."

He disappeared along the passage. After a short hesitation, Tanya followed. Gill was left standing there by herself. She had never felt so useless, so unwanted. That Nicky—Nicky, of all people—should be in need of comfort and she deliberately excluded—Derek could go to him, Tanya could go to him: she alone must be barred. She, who ought to be there putting her arms round him, telling him how she loved him, how desperately sorry she was—

"Because I *am* sorry, Nicky, I am, I truly am!"

The tears pricked at her eyes as she stood there. Sooner a thousand times have the boy still alive and Nicky happy than that he should be dead and Nicky suffering. Why, oh, why, had she hated him so much? What harm had he ever done her? It hadn't been his fault. And Nicky had loved him, and there was nothing she could do, nothing she could say, that would ever make up for the way that she had treated him.

"Gill—" It was Kath, hurrying towards her, homely face full of concern. "I've just heard—oh, Gilly!" She caught at her hand. Rare indeed for Kath to be demonstrative. "Be kind to him. He loved that boy so much. Whatever you might have thought . . . he did love him. Try to be just a little sorry. Promise me, Gilly— don't do anything to hurt him. Not now."

How could she think it? How could she *think* it? Her lip trembled slightly.

"I'll be kind to him," she said. "If he'll let me . . ."

She left Kath and walked slowly on down the corridor by herself to Nicky's dressing room. Alex was still in there, she could hear. For her to go in would be to intrude where she could not possibly be welcome. Alex was the only person, at such a moment, whom he would want to have near him. Looking back on their lives she realized it was always Alex to whom they had turned: Alex, rather than

each other. She would be kind to him—
if only he would let her.

Several people passed by as she stood
waiting there. They walked on tiptoe, as
if in a hospital, scared of making any
untoward noise. They had, quite obviously, heard the news. István, Zoë,
Danielle, all three stopped to ask her the
same question: "How is he?" She had to
admit she didn't know—she hadn't yet
seen him. Madame came up, looked for a
second as if she were about to enter, then
hearing voices said: "Who has he in
there? Alex? In that case, I leave him.
And you, child—" she nodded briskly,
not altogether unsympathetically, at Gill
—"try to remember that in this moment
his pain is more than yours."

The door opened at last and Alex reappeared. She searched his face, rather
timidly.

"Is he—all right?"

"All right?" He spoke, for Alex, quite
roughly. "Would you *expect* him to be all
right? Would *you* be all right if someone
you were close to had just got himself run

over and killed? No, you wouldn't. You'd
be distressed at the very least. Well, so
is he." He jerked his thumb over his
shoulder. "Go in there and say something
to him."

She started back, nervously.

"Alex, I can't, I—"

"I said, *go in there!*"

He caught her by the shoulder and
dragged her towards the door. She looked
up at him, piteously.

"Alex—"

How could *she* go in there? She, who
had all along refused to be reconciled, had
rejected every peace offer that Nicky had
ever made? She had forfeited all right.
How could *she* go in there *now?*

She did not have to. Before she could
make any move, the door had opened
again and Nicky himself had come out.
She was standing so close that he almost
tripped over her.

"Excuse me," he said.

He made to walk past her. Just in time,
the words blurted themselves out:

"Nicky, I'm sorry about Gino—"

It was the first time she had ever referred to him by name. She realized it even as she said it: the word sounded stiff and strained on her lips. There was a fractional pause. For a moment she thought he was going to make no acknowledgement of any kind; then faintly, very faintly, he inclined his head towards her as he went on his way down the passage.

"Well, at least you tried," said Alex. He made it very obvious he didn't think much of her effort.

9

THE theatre was not the same without Gino. As Tanya said, he had been so quiet, just sitting there in his corner with his sketch-book and his pencil, you scarcely realized how much a part of the place he had become until he was no longer there.

"He was always so *happy*—it seems so unfair. It seems so cruel. All he ever wanted was to be with Nicky and to get on with his drawing."

If it seemed unfair to Tanya—if it seemed cruel to her—how much more so must it seem to Nicky? Impossible, thought Alex, not to feel for the boy. Impossible not to be concerned about him. He had taken it, at the time, too well. He had been too stoical. He had gone on and danced that night just as if nothing had ever happened, had refused, despite all Alex's entreaties, to return afterwards to Clapham with himself and Gill.

"I wish you would . . . I don't like the idea of you going back to an empty flat."

"No," Nicky had said, somewhat wryly. "I can't say I'm too crazy at the prospect myself."

"Then why not give it a miss just for tonight? Mm? Come back home with us . . . please, Nicky."

He wouldn't; neither then nor later. For the next two weeks, which were all that were left of their London season, he had been subdued, but seemed to be coping. Everyone in the Company had been shaken in some degree or another by what had occurred. For what it was worth, there was no lack of sympathy. Tanya, in particular, had gone out of her way to ensure that he knew it. She had always had a soft spot for Nicky. She fussed over him now like a mother hen: Derek bore with it nobly, in silence. As for Gill, timidly she did her best to demonstrate that all past hostility was repented of, that she, as much as anyone, appreciated the nature of his loss. Nicky did not exactly reject her advances, simply he seemed to derive no comfort from them. It was in Tanya's arms he sought relief, not Gill's. Alex could understand the anguish she must feel, having to stand by and watch another give him the solace that he either could not or would not accept from her, but only time, at this stage, could heal the breach between them. The rift had gone too deep to be closed up overnight.

Towards the end of January, they went on tour. He had hoped the change of scene might help, that it would do the boy good to be away from London, away from the desolate flat, away even from the theatre, but it seemed only to trigger off a delayed reaction. Usually the most outgoing of persons, Nicky became, almost overnight, reserved, remote, un-approachable. He who had always responded so readily to any demonstration of affection now shrank from all form of contact, be it either mental or physical. Tanya alone seemed still able to reach him. He would suffer from her what he would suffer from no one else. Tanya might go up and put her arms round him if she wished, she might kiss him and pet him and generally make a fuss of him: only let anyone else attempt it and they were very quickly shrugged off.

"God knows," said Derek, "I'd sooner have him talking nineteen to the dozen and driving us all demented than like this."

So, too, would everyone. They had complained often enough in the past that it was like trying to work with a mechanical jack-in-the-box, that he never kept still, never kept quiet, never gave anyone a moment's peace, but it was as if, now, a light had gone out. Life might be less hectic: it was also a great deal less fun.

Out of working hours, he was scarcely ever seen. He had always been prone to the odd disappearing act, going off by himself with no one for company; now he vanished for long periods at a stretch, slipping out of the theatre the minute the evening performance was over, not

turning up again until two or three
o'clock in the morning. On several
occasions, Alex had good cause to
suspect, he had not come back to the
hotel all night. One Sunday morning,
travelling up from Portsmouth to
Southampton, they had been forced to
leave without him. No one had seen him
since half-past ten the previous night.
Derek had looked in on him in his
dressing room to say "Coming for a bite
to eat?" and he had said no, he wasn't
hungry, he'd see them back at the hotel,
in the bar. They'd sat in the bar until past
midnight, but he had never shown up.
His key had still been downstairs at the
reception desk when they went for breakfast next morning. Gill, biting her lip, had
said: "Where do you think he's got to?"
Alex preferred, at that moment, quite
frankly, not to have to think. He hunched
a shoulder.

"We—we shouldn't ring the police?"

"He's a big boy, Gilly. You can't get
the police out because a grown man
chooses to spend a night on the tiles."

"But he—he might have—"

"Might have what?"

"Might have—"

Thrown himself into the harbour? Jumped under a train? Were those the fears that haunted her? Strangely, such possibilities had not until this moment occurred to him—because perhaps he knew so well that it was not that particular type of oblivion that the boy was seeking. He stretched out a consoling hand across the breakfast table.

"He'll be all right. Don't worry yourself . . . he'll turn up." He did turn up —six hours later, in a taxi all the way from Portsmouth, red-eyed, unshaven, looking, in general, more than a little the worse for wear. Alex refrained from asking him where he had spent the night. Wherever it was, it had done precious little for him. He evidently felt so himself: for the whole of the following week, he was a model of chastity, sobriety, and early nights in bed. No Cistercian monk could have led a life more blameless than Nicky's. It was, of course, too good to last. Just as Alex had begun to cherish real hopes that the restless urge which possessed him had finally and definitely burnt itself out, he started again on his wanderings. Again, lying awake in hotel beds at two o'clock, at three o'clock, Alex would toss and turn wondering where the boy was, whether he were yet back, whether they would find him there in the morning. He tried his best to make light of it to Gill, saying it was "a natural reaction, he'll get over it, just let him be", but in truth it worried him, this perpetual roaming of the streets in search of heaven knows what. He was not going to find solace that way—was far more likely to run into a whole cartload of trouble. Apart from anything else, there were the sheer physical dangers to which he was exposing himself. He was a bonny enough fighter in a scrap, as Alex from experience could too well testify, but he would be no match at all for some of the types that peopled that twilight wilderness through which he was wont to take his nightly perambulations.

What could one do? He could not keep the boy on a leash. He could only try talking sense into him, and he doubted very much that he was yet in any emotional state to listen. He made the attempt, nevertheless, mincing no words, pointing out to him with unflinching brutality that a series of squalid affairs with every Tom, Dick and Harry picked up off the street corner was not going to bring him another Gino. Nicky said savagely that he did not want another Gino: it was too much heartbreak. From now on, he was going to "take it where he could find it."

It was a phase that would pass, even as grief itself would pass; it did nothing, in the meanwhile, to dispel anxiety.

They returned to London at the end of March. Rehearsals started once again for *Adam*. He had had doubts, himself, as to the wisdom of it—unless, perhaps, with a change of cast. Madame said firmly that she would "make no concessions". She was well aware that Gill and Nicky had had their problems—was well aware of the nature of those problems; but if Gino's death had done nothing else it had at least brought Gill to her senses. As for Nicky, she was as sorry for him as anyone, but the boy was a professional, work must come first, and through work alone would he find his salvation.

"*Quant à toi, mon Alex—*" she touched his cheek lightly with one slender finger—"I know well enough how you feel. I know, believe me, what I am asking of you—to teach the rôle to another and not to dance it yourself . . . *je le sais bien*. It is not easy. But *courage, mon vieux* . . . remember that you, too, are a professional. Work must be the only thing that counts."

If he could not wholeheartedly endorse the latter sentiment, he could scarcely dispute the basic premise: personal feelings must be put to one side if the job were to be done successfully. He embarked with no very great faith on the task, but Madame, after all, had not been running her own company for almost a quarter of a century without learning something of her dancers' psychology. Gill came to the part of Temptation without a trace of her former difficulties. It was as if, having finally accepted Nicky as he was and not as she would have liked him to be, she could approach the rôle with the same objectivity as she approached any other, without that element of intense personal identification which before had so crippled her. Nicky himself was working as well as ever he had. One had to hand it to the boy. Whatever the storm-tossed nature of his private life, his professional one, at any rate, he maintained on an even keel. He might arrive for morning class looking like a hell upon earth, but he always, and punctually, arrived. Off-stage, though no longer uncommunicative, he yet had none of that irrepressible sparkle that had enlivened so many a dull hour, had shattered so many a peaceful moment. In performance, in public, he appeared exactly the same high-spirited, swashbuckling Nicky that he had always been. Watching his Harlequin, his Mercutio, his Franz, one would never have guessed at the inner turmoil.

There came a morning, a Monday morning, when he was not there. No one could ever remember Nicky to have missed class before. He had been there with the flu, he had been there with a broken bone and a wrist done up in plaster. Now he had not even telephoned to make his excuses: from the flat in Guilford Street Alex could get no reply. István volunteered the information that he had seen Nicky the previous night, very briefly, in the Hereford. He had been drinking, but he certainly had not been drunk. He had seemed in reasonably good spirits. When Alex asked if he had been with anyone, István looked uncomfortable and muttered only that he "might have been . . . I didn't stay long, you know?" From all that one had heard of it, the Hereford was not, these days—if indeed it had ever been—a particularly salubrious spot in which to spend one's Sunday evening. Perhaps when class were over it might be wise just to pop round to the flat and check on the situation. He asked Gill if he might have her key, but it appeared she no longer had one; and what did he want it for, anyway? On hearing that he was going round to the flat, she instantly declared her intention of going with him. He told her no. They had quite a tussle over it.

"*Why* can't I?"

"Because I say you can't, that's why."

"Alex, I'm not a child, you know. I'm perfectly well aware of what goes on in that place."

"What place?"

"*That* place . . . the Hereford. I wanted to go there once. He wouldn't take me. He—"

"Oh, wouldn't he? Well, that shows he's obviously got more sense of propriety than I gave him credit for."

"As a matter of fact, he said *you* wouldn't like it."

"He's damned right I wouldn't. If he chooses to go there himself, that's up to him, there's nothing very much that I can do about it, but—"

"But you're not going there *now*, you're going round to the flat, and I don't see why I shouldn't be allowed to come with you. Suppose something's happened to him? I do love him, you know—just as much as you do."

Alex gave a faint, sardonic smile. Where had he heard those words before? *I do love her, you know . . . just as much as you do*. He sometimes wondered why he bothered with the troublesome pair, the number of headaches they caused him.

He refused to be browbeaten by her. He insisted she remain at the theatre, and was glad enough, in the event, that he had. At first, when he rang the bell, there was no answer. He felt with sinking heart that the place was deserted, but he tried again anyway, this time pushing at the flap of the letter box, as well, and calling through it: "Nicky . . . are you there?"

Seconds later, Nicky appeared at the door. He was staggering and had his dressing gown half clutched round him. His forehead and the whole of one side of his face were caked with dry blood. Alex stared at him, aghast.

"What in God's name—"

Nicky swayed slightly.

"S time?"

"Getting on for eleven. What the—"

"*Eleven?*" He put a hand to his forehead and winced. "Damn! Means I've missed class."

"To hell with the poxy class! What I want to know is what the devil you've been doing to yourself?"

"Haven't been doing anything to myself . . . don't think *I*'d go round cracking half the top of my skull open, do you? Not a flaming masochist."

"Then who the—oh, never mind! Come in here and let's take a look at you."

He shut the front door and helped the boy through to the sitting-room. Above his right eye, extending into the hairline, was a jagged hole, oozing even now a thin trickle of blood. Alex shook his head.

"You're going to need a quack for this. It looks like a needle and thread job. Even if it's not, you're going to be left with a nice scar . . . Have you—er—sustained any other injuries?"

Nicky grimaced.

"What do you want? Blood? There's already enough around to float a battleship."

"You can say that again. Just hang on where you are, I'll see if I can't get you cleaned up a bit."

There was not a great deal he could do. As he had said, the wound required medical attention, he could only sponge away the dried blood round the edges. He made a cup of tea, went through to the bedroom to fetch some clothes for the boy, found the place a shambles. There was a large bloodstain on the top blanket. It had soaked right through two more layers and both sheets to the mattress. He pulled a face and went back out to the sitting-room, where Nicky, huddled before the fire, was cradling his mug of tea between his hands.

"That was given to you," said Alex, "to drink, not to cuddle."

Nicky took a sip.

"*Merde!* You've put sugar in it!"

"Of course I've put sugar in it. I didn't spend three years in the Boy Scouts for nothing. Hot sweet tea in case of shock? Drink it up. It's good for you."

"I loathe things that are good for me—in any case, I'm not shocked."

"Well, you flaming well ought to be, that's all I can say! Get it down you and shut up."

In mutinous silence, Nicky drank his tea. As he helped him on with his clothes, Alex said: "What do we do? Call the law?"

"You must be joking!"

"Why? You haven't committed any crime, have you?"

"Don't be cretinous . . . that's not the point."

"So what is? The fact that you've gone and got yourself beaten up? The—"

"Do you hear me complaining? You run risks, you have to take the consequences." He shrugged. "So sometimes they're not always so pleasant."

Alex forbore, for the time being, to point out that there were some risks which were not only unacceptable but also totally unnecessary; he would tackle that aspect later. Just at present there were more urgent details pressing for attention. He rang Gill at the theatre to tell her that Nicky was all right, that he had just "come home a bit hit and missed and knocked himself cold tripping over his own feet". She accepted the story, even while making it plain that she did not believe a word of it. He was not very surprised. If there were one fault (perhaps the *only?*) that Nicky did not possess, it was that of drinking to excess. Even if he had, he were far too fleet of foot to go tripping over himself. She was tactful enough, however, for the moment, to refrain from pushing inquiries too far.

Alex fetched the car from its underground parking place, bundled a still slightly dazed Nicky down the stairs, drove him straight off to the nearest casualty department. He escaped the disfigurement of stitches, the wound for all its ugliness was not as deep as at first appeared, but there could clearly be no question of his going on that night. It was that which seemed to cause him more anxiety than all the rest put together. Being hit on the head by some psychopath or common-or-garden thug he could take in his stride: being banned from dancing for only twenty-four hours threw him into instant agitation. Of course he could dance! What did the fool think he was talking about? A couple of aspirins and a bit of sticking plaster and he would be right as rain. For crying out loud! You couldn't go letting people down for a mere tuppeny-ha'penny scratch on the head.

"It's not a mere tuppeny-ha'penny scratch, it's a filthy great hole, and furthermore you've been out for the count for God knows how long . . . If you don't want to find yourself laid up for the rest of the week, then just do as you're told and accept for once that someone knows better than you do."

There was, in any case, no call for

panic. The ballet scheduled for that evening was *Coppélia*. Franz was a rôle which he himself had danced often enough in the past—not, admittedly, for some little while, but he could quite easily take over for just the one night.

"You don't have to bother yourself on that particular score." Far more important was the pattern of his own future behaviour. "You can't carry on like this, Nicky. I don't care how chewed up you're feeling, emotionally, that's no excuse for this sort of thing. What are you trying to do? Commit suicide? Because you go on as you've been doing just lately and sooner or later you're either going to get yourself run in or done in, one or the other—and I tell you, frankly, the prospect of having to come and bail you out the nick grabs me no more than the prospect of having to identify your body at the morgue, so—"

"Digit extractum . . . don't worry. I'm not a complete nut case. Even I, at last, begin to have some faint glimmerings of the fact that the time might have come to draw a line."

"It's not as if anyone expects you to live like a Buddhist monk."

"Why not? Might not be such a bad idea at that."

"For a short while, I make no doubt, it would be an extremely good idea."

"I meant," said Nicky, "on a rather more permanent sort of basis."

Alex shot him a quick glance.

"There's no need to go to extremes."

"What's extreme about it? Other people do it; why shouldn't I?"

"Because you're a bloody good dancer! Don't talk arrant rubbish. I know you're going through a bad patch just at the moment, but believe me, kiddo, things will get better. They always do. Just give it time. It will pass, I promise you."

"Yes, and when it has, what then? What's left? A vacuum? It's not so easy trying to re-learn how to exist just for yourself.

Alex thought: *that I should have lived*

to hear him tell me that . . . Aloud, after a few seconds' internal struggle, he said:

"Would it be of any help, do you think, if Gill were to move back in with you?"

Nicky said neither yes nor no, but only:

"She must have been glad, at any rate."

"Glad?"

"The day it happened."

"Of course she wasn't glad!" He spoke sharply. "That's a disgraceful thing to say. She was just as upset for you as anyone, probably even more so."

"That was only because she hated him. You always feel guilty if you hate someone and then—then that happens."

"Nicky, she did not hate him. She was hurt, she was screwed up, she felt you'd let her make a fool of herself, but just get it out of your head that she hated him."

"He always felt that she did. He wanted to be friends with her, but she wouldn't."

"She would have come round to it, Nicky. Sooner or later. She never stopped loving you. It was only *because* she loved you . . . she'd move back in with you tomorrow, if you were to ask her."

"Oh, for God's sake! What good do you think I'd be to her? In any case, just try thinking of yourself, for a change. You've wet-nursed us for long enough—it's your turn now. You want to lose her just as you're coming up to the winning post? Stick with it, you fool! Don't worry yourself about me, I'll survive, one way or the other. I may take a few knocks while I'm doing it, but I'll still be around. You look after number one, and sod the rest of us. You want that girl, you go and get her. She's had the kid glove treatment for long enough. A bit of the old rape and pillage wouldn't do her any harm."

Alex smiled—Nicky was a fine one to be lecturing him! There might, perhaps, have been a grain of truth in what the boy said, but one could not change one's image overnight. Gill, he knew, could have been his for the asking any time these past few months. There had been not a few occasions when he had been sorely tempted. If he had resisted the impulse, it had been because her thoughts even now were all channelled in Nicky's direction. Unless and until the day ever came that she wanted *him*, for *himself* —

"She does love you, you know."

He laughed at that: he couldn't help it.

"Just as much as you do, I suppose!"

Nicky wrinkled his brow.

"What are you talking about?"

"Never mind . . . it's just my own private joke!"

The old maid of a doctor, poncing about in his white coat playing at God, had instructed him to spend the rest of the day at home, "taking things quietly".

"You're lucky to get away without stitches. I ought by rights to keep you in for twenty-four hours, but—"

But they had at least spared him that. Shortage of beds, no doubt—and anyway, it was ridiculous, he felt perfectly fit. A bit groggy, perhaps, but hardly a stretcher case. He could have gone on and danced, had it really been necessary.

Alex, plainly not trusting him, had insisted on remaining with him until it was time to go back to the theatre for the evening performance. His parting injunction, as he left, was:

"Just make sure you stay put . . . I've half a mind to send Manuela up to keep an eye on you."

"That wouldn't be any rest cure—she'd rape me as soon as look at me. I'm terrified to be alone with her for more than five seconds."

"Well, all right, but don't get up to anything stupid."

"Oh, come off it, Alex! What do you think I'm going to do? Go out looking for more trouble the minute your back's turned?"

"No, I'm sure you're not as daft as that. But just remember you've got a first night coming up in a week's time. That ballet's been fated enough as it is. I don't want it postponed all over again."

He did his best to obey instructions, but taking things quietly was not in his nature, and the empty flat, in any case, had become anathema to him—especially on a night when he ought by rights to have been at the theatre himself. He stuck it for an hour; it was as much as he could tolerate. He knew, after that, that he had to get out. If he stayed any longer, the nightmares would start. He had tried it before. He had tried sitting it out, forcing himself by sheer will power to remain behind closed doors. He had watched God knows what kind of rubbish stuff on the box, all the way through till shut-down, in an attempt to keep his mind diverted from other channels. It was only a delaying tactic. It held at bay, but could not finally eradicate. It made it, if anything, even worse when it actually came.

Tanya had said why didn't he ask the doctor for some sleeping tablets. She said everybody needed help at some time in their lives: "You can't be expected to go it alone. Not when a thing like this hits you." But *sleeping* tablets? The world had surely come to a sorry pass if they were to provide a substitute for the warmth of human contact. Had all been well between himself and Gill—had they been on their old terms—he might then have found some comfort in doing what Alex had wanted him to do, going home again for a while; but how could he, with things as they were? He had treated Gill dismally. He could not escape responsibility. That he had never intended it was neither here nor there. Had he not been so bound up in his own concerns, he must surely have seen for himself, long, long ago, before all the damage had been done, the way it was with her. In truth, he ought never to have allowed her to move in with him. It had been the purest unthinking selfishness on his part. He had been lonely without Vic—perhaps, too, a little resentful? Feeling himself abandoned? Vic had found Trudi, he had had no one. Gill had filled the gap admirably —or seemed to do so. As Alex had said, *I suppose you imagined you could carry on just the same as usual? Just carry on amusing yourself the same as if she wasn't there?*

It was, to his shame, precisely what he had imagined. Now they were both paying the price for it. Alex said that she loved him still, and God knows he loved her. He had never stopped doing so, not for a moment. But how, after all that had occurred, were they ever to tell each other?

He shifted restlessly about the flat. He had promised Alex there would be no more nightly wanderings, and it was a promise he intended to honour; but how, for pity's sake, was he expected to remain here all evening with nothing but his own thoughts to bear him company? There was drink, of course; but drink was no way out. Drugs, too—but what went up had to come down, and the higher you flew the harder you fell. The shattering jolt of the return to reality was too high a price to pay for a few short hours of psychedelic obliteration. There were always Vic and Trudi. He could go to them any time he liked, day or night, they had told him often enough, *Don't hesitate, just drop everything and come.*

There'll always be a bed here for you, you know that.

He did know it. The *Drei Sterne*, once, had been almost like a second home—but for that very reason it held too many memories. It would be some time, yet, before he could bring himself to go back there again. But he had, for God's sake, to go *some*where. Suppose he were to slip down the road to the theatre to spend a busman's holiday watching the ballet? Even Alex, surely, could not object to that?

No sooner thought about than put into practice. Within twenty minutes he had purchased his ticket, incognito, like any other member of the public, and was sitting out front, theatrically hiding behind dark glasses with his coat collar turned up, head buried in programme, waiting along with everyone else for the house lights to dim. He heard the announcement that he himself would not be able to appear that night owing to "indisposition" and that his place would be taken by Alex. It was many years since he had seen Alex dance the role of Franz. It was not, now, the sort of part that one would readily identify him with—it required too boisterous a sense of fun, a devil-may-care-ness that did not, on the face of it, accord with those qualities of rocklike steadiness and sterling dependability that had come to be associated with him. He found himself quite anxious on Alex's behalf—and realized, also, that this would be the first time he had ever seen him partner Gill in any major rôle. They had danced together occasionally, just very occasionally, in more minor pieces, but never in leading rôles in a full-length ballet. It would be interesting, if nothing else, to see how the evening went.

It was more than interesting. It was, to Nicky, something of an eye opener. Gill, as ever, was a delight as Swanilda: pert, petite and mischievous, yet always with that slightly withdrawn quality that singled her out, set her apart from her fellows. She responded to Alex as if they had been dancing together all their lives. Watching her, Nicky could tell that she not only had complete faith in him, as indeed must anyone who knew him, but over and above that there was between them an instinctive understanding and sympathy which owed nothing to mere technical skill. That, perhaps, was not so very surprising. Alex had certainly been in love with Gill for at least the whole of his adult life, if not even before. As for her, he was inclined to think her feelings rather stronger than she herself had any inkling of. Had she not been the first, as a child, to rush to Alex's defence? Had she not stuck up for him even against the adored cousin who—he had been aware of it even then—could make any demands upon her that he wished? Had not Alex been the very first person she had wanted to see on their return home from abroad? *He* had not gone racing off straightaway to Clapham: he had preferred to amuse himself in pursuits of his own, going out to Chalk Farm to see Vic and Trudi, meeting for the first time a boy who for better or for worse was going to change the entire selfish pattern of his twenty-four years of life. It would never have occurred to him to spend his first evening back paying a visit to Alex: it would never have occurred to Gill to spend her first evening back doing anything other. Small wonder, then, she should blossom so readily for him as Swanilda.

What was far more of a revelation was Alex's portrayal of Franz. He disclosed that night aspects of himself which Nicky had not known him to possess. If perhaps essential innocence were missing, there was no lack of humour or high spirits. It was a Franz not quite so boyish as Nicky's, a Franz who had been around a bit, had done and seen a thing or two, but nonetheless persuasive on that account. Alex, when required, could obviously charm an audience as well as anyone. He could clown and fool and make believe. Why he did not do so more often was a puzzle, until one reflected that he was rarely if ever given the opportunity. He had lived for too long in the shadow of Nicky's more obvious virtuosity. At too early an age he had accepted responsi-

bilities, and too zealously had he carried
them out. If he had only devoted himself
a little more to his own interests, and a
little less to those of Gill and Nicky, it
might have been he, now, who was
looking forward to that opening night of
Adam only one week away. It could not
help but give one food for speculation.

Nicky left the theatre as soon as the
curtain went down on the final *galop*, the
bells ringing with the approach of dusk.
He slipped out as he had come in, unsung
and unmarked. That night was the first
night, for a very long time, on which he
actually found himself able to return to
the empty flat, to open the front door and
walk inside, without his thoughts automatically reverting to the one subject that
so excruciatingly obsessed him. It was the
first night on which he was not instantly
assailed by that searing pain which had of
late made the place almost unendurable to
him: the first night on which he did not
feel impelled by torturing insomnia to go
back out and tramp the streets in search
of some kind of forgetfulness. Instead, he

went straight to his bed and slept right through till morning; and when he woke, he knew, with absolute certainty, with a clarity he had never had before, what it was that he was going to do.

10

PANIC backstage: thirty minutes to curtain up on the first night of *Adam* and Nicky had gone and passed out on them. He had never done such a thing in his life before. He was just not the sort of person who passed out. It was not even as if the opening ballet had required anything particularly strenuous of him. Had it been *Tricorne* or *Prince Igor*—but all it was was *Nuages*, an innocuous little piece if ever there was one, gentle and dreamy, set to Debussy *Préludes*. Alex and Andrea had danced the leads; Nicky had scarcely been on stage for more than ten minutes. He had taken his curtain call along with everyone else, seemed perfectly all right, gone back to his dressing-room for the interval—and now this.

Of course, it was the bash on the head which had done it—that mysterious bash on the head which was supposed to have been caused by an excess of alcohol and an ignominious tripping over of his own feet. Gill had not believed it at the time, she did not believe it now. She knew well enough that Alex was hiding something from her; she could make a fair guess what it was. She had not pressed him for details. He had assured her there was no cause for alarm: "It needed an incident like this to bring him to his senses. It's not something he'll let happen again in a hurry." Without any doubt, aching head or not, Nicky this past week had seemed far brighter, far more like his old resilient self. *She* had only queried whether he ought to have started dancing again quite as quickly as he did, but as Alex had pointed out, it was better for him to be here at the theatre, in the midst of things, than brooding at home in an empty flat.

"I shouldn't worry too much about him. He's pretty indestructible."

Certainly he had seemed so. He had taken but the twenty-four hours off then turned up next day with a strip of sticking plaster adorning his forehead, a cheerful grin, and the defiant announcement that he was "as fit as a fiddle and ready for anything". The doctor, apparently, had given the go-ahead, so there really was no arguing with him. In any case, Nicky was tough: it would take more than a cracked skull to keep him out of action. So, at least, they had thought. Now when he was most needed it had chosen to catch up on him.

He should have spent the week at home, she had said so all along. They should have kept him in the hospital, they should have X-rayed him. For all they knew, he could have a fracture—he could be suffering from delayed concussion, could even, God forbid, have a blood clot. Limbering up at the barre, trying not to dwell too much on all the manifold complications that *could* have assailed him, Gill had no idea whether to prepare herself for *Adam* or for yet another post-ponement. It would not be so easy, at this stage in the evening and with half the Company already departed, to bring in a substitute work. But with Nicky out of commission—She heard her name spoken and turned, quickly.

"Yes, Madame?"

"All is well, child. We go ahead."

Her heart lifted.

"He's all right?"

"He is back to consciousness, but not to dance. There are too many lifts—too dangerous. If he were to drop you—" She shook her head. "I cannot allow."

"Then who—"

"Alex," said Madame. "You will dance with Alex."

"*Alex?*"

"And why not?" The eyebrows raised themselves in faint, aristocratic disapproval. "Does he not know the part as well as Nicky? Is he not the one who has taught it to him? Why then do you say *Alex* like this?"

"I'm sorry, Madame." Her cheeks coloured. "I just—didn't expect it, that was all."

"You did not expect it, he did not expect it. He will need all the help that you can give him. Be sure you do not let him down. It means much to him.”

“Yes, Madame.”

She dropped a slight curtsey. Madame nodded.

“It will go well. *Bonne chance*, my little one.”

With a careless pat on the cheek, Madame continued stately onwards. Gill turned and scampered off in the opposite direction. She looked in on Alex to wish him good luck: he pulled a face and said, “I’ll need it.” She laughed.

“False modesty will get you nowhere!” As Madame had said, did he not know the part every bit as well as Nicky? Was he not the very one who had taught it to him? “Do it standing on your head!”

Nicky in turn dropped in upon her.

“I’m going out front to see how it looks from the other side . . . you’d better make sure it’s worth watching!”

She eyed him with some concern.

“Oughtn’t you to be in bed, or lying down?”

“What? And miss all the fun? No

way!" He bent and dropped a kiss on her forehead. "Best of luck, sweetheart."

"Oh, Nicky—" She gazed up at him with troubled eyes. "After all the work we've put in . . . it does seem unfair."

"Not unfair. Brought it on myself, didn't I? As Alexis so rightly pointed out, if I will behave like an irresponsible cretin—"

"He never said that!"

"Well . . . perhaps not, but he might have done. I'd have accepted it. Anyway, it gives him a chance for once to show what he can do. You take good care of him out there—you treat him nicely. I don't want either of you letting me down."

She put the finishing touches to her make-up, powdered it off, readjusted her shoe ribbons, stood there for a moment studying herself in the glass. Blood-red tights and scarlet leotard, raven hair pulled back from narrow face with its exaggerated ballet make-up—was she tempting enough? Was she exotic? She looked to her own critical eye like a virgin waif in wolf's clothing, like a nun got up for a fancy dress ball. She didn't care what Alex said: it *was* a fight against nature. How could she, in all earnestness, be expected to tempt anyone? She had certainly not tempted *him* during these last months while she had been living at home. He had taken even less notice of her that way than Nicky. With Nicky she didn't mind; not now that she knew. Dancing with him, she had managed at last to come to terms with the ballet, for after all they were both of them playing a part. If Nicky could convince as Adam, there was no reason why she should not do likewise as Temptation. But with Alex—Alex, who made love to voluptuous French sirens like Danielle—small wonder he paid scant attention to *her*. What had she to offer him? Just a bag of skin and bones . . .

Well, it couldn't be helped. She would go out there and she would do her best. You didn't have to be mentally deranged to dance Giselle; why then should you have to have sex appeal to dance Temptation?

She arrived in the wings to find Alex already there, waiting. He had pushed his bare feet into a pair of old ballet slippers and had his bath robe wrapped round him. She said:

"How are you feeling?"

He grinned, but none too easily.

"Like a dowager about to take an early morning dip in front of ten thousand interested onlookers."

"Are you *shy?*"

She made, teasingly, to put her arms round him, but he backed away, nervously.

"Don't do that, you stupid girl!"

"Why not? What's the matter?"

"Just have a bit of consideration, for Pete's sake . . . You're meant to be seducing me *on* stage, not off."

"I didn't think I was capable of seducing you at all."

"I don't know what gave you that idea!"

"You mean that I *am?*"

"Just come one step closer and you've practically done it."

She smiled, mischievously.

"You don't think we should maybe have a practice run?"

"Like hell!"

She was about to make yet another jokey remark when it struck her, quite suddenly, that Alex was not playacting: he really and truly was scared. The realization sobered her. *Alex? Scared?* He was always so cool, so calm, so competent. He was always the one who was offering comfort and assurance to everyone else. He was the one to whom everyone, automatically, turned. He *couldn't* be scared.

But he was; very obviously.

"Oh, *Alex!*" She slid both arms round his neck. This time, he did not back away from her. She felt him shiver slightly. "You're not cold?"

He shook his head.

"No."

Not cold, just paralysed by nerves. Madame must have known. What was it she had said? *He will need all the help you can give him* . . . Nicky, too—*you take good care of him* out there. You treat him nicely —

"Alex, you've danced it a hundred times with me in rehearsal," she said.

"That still doesn't make me into a Nicky, does it?"

"So what if it doesn't? You're you. Isn't that good enough?"

He made no reply. She stood with her arms clasped round his neck, looking up at him. *This is Alex*, she thought. *Alex, to whom I owe almost everything . . . Alex, whom for far too long I have just taken for granted* . . . If he were no longer there, however would she manage without him? If he were to marry tomorrow—a Kath, or worse by far, a Danielle—but no, not even a Kath! She would begrudge him even to her. As for Danielle—when had she last seen the two of them together? Months ago. Before Christmas? The day on which she had stumbled into the flat and found Nicky with Gino and gone running all the way back to Clapham to cry on Alex's shoulder: *that* was the last time she had seen them. So bound up had she been in her own woes, her own problems, she had never troubled herself to notice that the affair had come to an end. He surely could not have thrown her over only for Gill's sake, only because *she* had now come home to roost? But yet that first night back from tour—and had not Nicky said?—and then Kath? *I'm sure you could have, if you played your cards right* . . . But she didn't have any cards, she wasn't any good at card games—

"Oh, Alex!" she said. She went on tiptoe, arms still clasped about his neck. "Darling Alex, I do love you so very, very much . . ."

Nicky was there, waiting for her, in her dressing room when she got back. As soon as they were alone together, she said: "Well?"

He laughed.

"You don't need me to tell you . . . it went a treat and you know it."

"We didn't let you down?"

"Of course you didn't. I never imagined for one moment that you would. If I'd had the least fear of that, I'd—"

"You'd what?" She looked at him, suspiciously. "You'd *what?*"

"I'd—I'd never have passed out in the first place!"

"*Nicky*—"

Her tone was accusing. He grinned, half shamefaced, half defiant.

"I reckoned it was about time old Alexis had a break."

"But suppose it had all gone wrong for him? You were taking a chance!"

"No, I wasn't. I knew perfectly well that it wouldn't all go wrong—which is not to say, however, that you're at liberty to spill the beans. One word out of you, my girl—"

"I won't say anything! Of course I won't say anything! What do you take me for?"

"A big blabbermouth . . . I can just hear you. Five minutes after the light's out, snuggled down beneath the bedclothes . . . *He told me not to tell you, so don't ever let on that you know, but—*"

"But since, as you *may* perhaps remember, we happen to sleep at totally opposite ends of the passage—"

"Don't you kid yourself! After tonight? You might as well shut one room up right here and now and wait till you start needing it as a nursery . . . what are you blushing for? These things happen. You've got to admit, Alexis would make a lovely father."

"Not," said Gill, "for at *least* ten years."

"Well, don't leave it too long. I don't want to be middle-aged before I'm an uncle . . . *would* I be an uncle? Perhaps I could be a godfather—or wouldn't you think that quite suited? I'm not exactly a figure of moral rectitude, am I?"

"Oh, don't be so silly!"

"Is it silly? I thought it bothered you."

"*That* didn't bother me. Not that in itself. It was only—"

"Yes, I know . . . I know." He held out a hand. "Gilly—am I forgiven?"

"You are if I am."

"Nothing to forgive you, sweetheart."

"Yes, there is. I was hateful."

"Wasn't your fault. Give us a kiss and tell me that you love me."

She went to him readily enough.

"I love you, Nicky . . . I do hope things work out for you."

"They will. One of these days. But if by any chance they don't—I've always got you and Alex, haven't I?"

"Yes." She held her face up for a kiss. "You've always got us."

The door opened and Alex appeared.

"For heaven's sake!" he said. "I thought you'd have been safely packed off home."

"Stayed on to see the show . . . just came round to express my approval."

"Oh, so that's what you call it, is it? Looked more like a bit of the old slap and tickle to me."

Nicky groaned.

"*Don't* say you're going to start getting all twisted and jealous like friend Derek

. . . I suppose I am allowed to kiss my own little cousin if I want?"

"Sure," said Alex. "Go ahead. Make a meal of it."

"Talking of meals—" Gently, Gill disengaged herself.

She went across to Alex. "I'm so hungry I could eat a horse."

"Tell me something new! Where do you want to go?"

"That place you took me to before? That place in Soho?"

"Why not? If you liked it—"

"It just seemed the right sort of atmosphere," said Gill, "in which to celebrate."

There was a pause. Alex held open the door.

"Come on, then," he said. "What are we waiting for?"

They both of them looked across at Nicky.

"Coming?" said Alex.

"Me? No, I—ah—I think I'd better be getting back home to bed. Have an early night. Don't want to go passing out on anyone again." He chivvied them both very firmly ahead of him down the passage to the stage door. "Off you go, children . . . enjoy yourselves. Do a whole lot of things that I wouldn't. See you in the morning. God bless . . ."

He waved them goodbye at the corner of the street, watched them walk away together towards the car park. Then he turned, in the direction of Guilford Street. At least for once in his life, he thought, he had actually done something right.

THE END

NURSE CAMDEN'S CAVALIER
Louise Ellis

The hospital was buzzing with rumours about the new Senior Surgical Registrar. Nurse Camilla Camden hadn't yet met him, but she thought he sounded a perfect horror. However she forgot all about him when she went to the hospital Fancy Dress Ball, and there met the Cavalier . . .

THE BELLS OF HEAVEN
Nan Herbert

Alex is sure she will never be happy again when her parents are killed in a road crash. But she makes her home on the East Coast with her uncle and eventually returns to the hospital as a staff nurse. There she meets Elizabeth who becomes both her friend and her enemy . . .

NURSE LORNA'S LOVE SONG
Kathleen Treves

When Lorna was jilted by her boyfriend Douglas, she thought she would never get over it. One of her patients suggested, half seriously, that she should pour out her heartbreak into a love song to get it out of her system. It did much more than that—it helped her to meet a man who could at last take Douglas's place.

THE BUTTERFLY AND THE BARON
Margaret Way

Renee Dalton was a rich society butterfly—but she didn't enjoy her artificial life. When cattle baron Nick Garbutt told her that she was frightened to feel she knew he was right, but what did it matter when Nick already had Sharon Russell, who was his for the asking?

THE PHYSICIANS
Elizabeth Harrison

The relationship between Nurse Anne Heseltine and Dr. Michael Vanstone was strange. Several times they had been on the verge of a deeper understanding. Anne knew that she was also loved by Bill Barham, and when a Professorship at the Central became vacant, Anne realised that the two men were becoming serious rivals—in work, and in love . . .

WITH ALL MY HEART
Christine Lawson

Housekeepers rarely stay long at Oakhill House. Austen Thurlow is troubled when Charlotte Gilroy tells him that she cannot take the post after all. Her brother and his wife have died, leaving two young sons whom Charlotte must look after. Austen is so desperate he tells her to bring the children with her. But soon after her arrival, Charlotte meets unexpected difficulties . . .

ROMANCE AT REDWAYS
Jane Lester

Darbie Ferris had been born with an insatiable itch to put things right for those people who were not as happy as she was. Kenward Marr, the new RSO at Redways, could have told her that people don't always want to be "fixed", but Darbie had to learn everything the hard way.

NURSE DOYLE IN DANGER
Jill Murray

Heartache threatens Nurse Thelma Doyle when the ex-girlfriend of RSO Gavin Yeomans returns to the hospital as a very sick patient. She is under the delusion that she is still engaged to Gavin, and, as she is so ill, Gavin goes along with this. Thelma does not see the danger signals until it is almost too late . . .

NEW DOCTOR AT NORTHMOOR
by Anne Durham

Doctor Mark Bayfield had managed to get on the wrong side of every member of the Kinglake family. But when young Gwenny Kinglake went into the hospital, Doctor Bayfield was the only man who was likely to diagnose the problem.

THE ENEMY WITHIN
by Nan Herbert

Marian undertakes to care for her young niece, but as she has also accepted a post as a Surgery Nurse, her fiancé, Hugh, protests, since Marian will have less time for him. When she receives an offensive anonymous letter, Marian suspects that Hugh might have written it!

REBEL IN LOVE
by Lilian Peake

Lex Moran, a man of considerable power, decided that the local school was uneconomic and should be closed down. But Katrine, the schoolteacher, felt passionately that the school should be saved, and she was determined to oppose Lex in every possible way.

NIGHT NURSE AT NASSINGHAM'S
by Quenna Tilbury

Christine Thorby was expected to become engaged to Dr. Peter Temscott, but the engagement never took place and Peter went to another hospital. It looked as though the same thing would happen when Martin Redway, the Surgical Registrar, fell in love with Christine . . .

DR. SIMON'S SECRET
by Kathleen Treves

Deborah Markham had just arrived to start her nursing training at Sappington General Hospital when she met Langdale Simon. Met him and fell in love, little knowing that he was the R.M.O. at the hospital where she would be working. But she was soon to find that loving Doctor Simon was not an easy matter . . .

LOVE FROM LINDA
by Kay Winchester

Nurse Linda Brooke, has no premonition of the impact on her life when three casualties arrive at the hospital late one night. They are Aurelle Boulton; a lorry driver with a shady past; and famous racing driver Cedric Deacon.

MASTER OF BEN ROSS
by Lucy Gillen

Melodie was enjoying her two months' painting holiday in the Highlands. She made some agreeable friends, in particular John Stirling—but most of all she was attracted and fascinated by the character of the local laird, Neil McDowell.

"YOU'LL MARRY MY CHOICE!"
by Christine Lawson

Sally Merridew knew that the lighthouse was her heritage but she hated the solitude and loneliness to which her watchful father subjected her. Even her friends were chosen for her, for he was a man who couldn't forget the past.

NURSE KATIE OF PRESSWOOD
by Jill Murray

Nurse Katie Holland is thrilled to hear that John Dancey, owner of an historic house, is planning to let some of it to make ends meet. She and the hospital almoner are delighted to make Presswood their new home.

SURETY FOR A STRANGER
by Mary Raymond

The lively, talented Shrewsbury family are haphazardly kind to Lewis Bellamore, a struggling young actor. He infiltrates their household and he takes something from each of them . . .